Tears Fall at

Night

Tears Fall at Night

Vanessa Miller

Book 1
Praise Him Anyhow Series

Vanessa Miller

www.vanessamiller.com

Printed in the United States of America
© 2013 by Vanessa Miller

Praise Unlimited Enterprises
Charlotte, NC

Other Books by Vanessa Miller

How Sweet The Sound
Heirs of Rebellion
The Best of All
Better for Us
Her Good Thing
Long Time Coming
A Promise of Forever Love
A Love for Tomorrow
Yesterday's Promise
Forgotten
Forgiven
Forsaken
Rain for Christmas (Novella)
Through the Storm
Rain Storm
Latter Rain
Abundant Rain
Former Rain

Anthologies (Editor)
Keeping the Faith
Have A Little Faith
This Far by Faith

EBOOKS

Love Isn't Enough

A Mighty Love

The Blessed One (Blessed and Highly Favored series)

The Wild One (Blessed and Highly Favored Series)

The Preacher's Choice (Blessed and Highly Favored Series)

The Politician's Wife (Blessed and Highly Favored Series)

The Playboy's Redemption (Blessed and Highly Favored Series)

Tears Fall at Night (Praise Him Anyhow Series)

Joy Comes in the Morning (Praise Him Anyhow Series)

A Forever Kind of Love (Praise Him Anyhow Series)

Ramsey's Praise (Praise Him Anyhow Series)

Escape to Love (Praise Him Anyhow Series)

Praise For Christmas (Praise Him Anyhow Series)

His Love Walk (Praise Him Anyhow Series)

One

"I'm leaving you," Judge Nelson Marshall said, as he walked into the kitchen and stood next to the stainless steel prep table.

Taking a sweet potato soufflé out of her brand new Viking, dual-baking oven, Carmella was bobbing her head to Yolanda Adams's, "I Got the Victory", so she didn't hear Nelson walk into the kitchen.

He turned the music down and said, "Did you hear me, Carmella? I'm leaving."

Carmella put the soufflé on her prep table and turned toward Nelson. He was frowning, and she'd never known him to frown when she baked his favorite soufflé. Then she saw the suitcase in his hand and understood. Nelson hated to travel. His idea of the perfect vacation was staying home and renting movies for an entire week, but recently he had been attending one convention after another. And last week, he'd been in Chicago with her as she had to attend her brother's funeral.

Carmella was thankful that Nelson had taken vacation to attend the funeral with her, because she really didn't think she would have made it through that week without him. She and her younger brother had always been close, but after losing both their parents by the time they were in their thirties, the bond between them had become even stronger. Now she was trying to make sense of a world where forty-six-year-old men died of heart attacks.

Nelson had been fidgety the entire time they were in Chicago. She knew he hated being away from home, so she cut their trip short by a day. He hadn't told her he had another trip planned. "Not another one of those boring political conventions?"

He shook his head.

Nelson had almost lost his last bid for criminal court judge. Since then he had been obsessed with networking with government officials in hopes of getting appointed to a federal bench and bypassing elections altogether.

"Sit down, Carmella, we need to talk."

Carmella sat down on one of the stools in front of the kitchen island.

Nelson sat down next to Carmella. He lowered his head.

"Nelson, what's wrong?"

He didn't respond. But he had the same look on his face that he'd had the night they'd received the call about his grandmother's death.

"Please say something, honey. You're scaring me," Carmella said.

He lifted his head and attempted to look into his wife's eyes, but quickly turned away as he said, "This doesn't work for me anymore."

Confused, Carmella asked, "What's not working?"

"This marriage, Carmella. It's not what I want anymore."

"I don't understand, Nelson." She turned away from him and looked around her expansive kitchen. It had been redesigned a couple of years ago to ensure that she had everything she needed to throw the most lavish dinner parties that Raleigh, NC had ever seen. Nelson had told her that if he were ever going to get an appointment to a federal bench, he would need to network and throw fundraising campaigns for the senators and congressmen of North Carolina.

So she'd exchanged her kitchen table for a prep table, and installed the walk-in cooler to keep her salads and desserts at just the right temperature for serving. The Viking stove with its six burners and dual oven—one side convection and the other with an infrared broiler—had been her most expensive purchase. But the oven had been worth it. The infrared broiler helped her food to taste like restaurant-quality broiled food, and the convection side of the oven did amazing things with her pastries. She'd turned her home into a showplace in order to impress the guests who attended their legendary dinner parties. She had done everything Nelson had asked her to do, so Carmella couldn't understand why she was now in her kitchen listening to her husband say that he didn't want this anymore. "We've been happy, right?"

Nelson shook his head. "I haven't been happy with our marriage for a long time now."

"Then why didn't you say something? We could have gone to counseling or talked with Pastor Mitchell."

Nelson stood up. "It's too late for that. I've already filed for a divorce. All you need to do is sign the papers when you receive them, and then we can both move on with our lives."

Tears welled in Carmella's eyes as she realized that while she had been living in this house and sleeping in the same bed with Nelson, he had been seeing a divorce lawyer behind her back. "What about the kids, Nelson? What am I supposed to tell them?"

"Our children are grown, Carmella. You can't hide behind them anymore."

"What's that supposed to mean?" Carmella stood up, anger flashing in her eyes. "Dontae is only seventeen years old. He's still in high school and needs both his parents to help him make his transition into adulthood."

"I'm not leaving Dontae. He can come live with me if he wants."

"Oh, so now you want to take my son away from me, too? What's gotten into you, Nelson? When did you become so cruel?"

"I'm not trying to take Dontae away from you. I just know that raising a son can be difficult for a woman to do alone. So, I'm offering to take him with me."

"That's generous of you," Carmella said snidely. Then a thought struck her, and she asked, "Are you seeing someone? Is that it? Is this some midlife crisis that you're going through?"

"This is not about anyone else, Carmella. It's about the fact that we just don't work anymore."

Tears were flowing down her honey-colored cheeks. "But I still love you. I don't want a divorce."

"I don't have time to argue with you. Just sign the papers and let's get this over with."

She put her hands on her small hips and did the sista-sista neck roll, as her bob-styled hair swished from one side to the other. "We haven't argued in years. I have just gone with the flow and done whatever you wanted me to do. But on the day my husband packs his bags and asks me for a divorce, I think we should at least argue about that, don't you?"

He pointed at her and sneered as if her very presence offended him. "See, this is exactly why I waited so long to tell you. I knew you were going to act irrational."

"Irrational! Are you kidding me?" Carmella wanted to pull her hair out. The man standing in front of her was not her husband. He must have fallen, bumped his head and lost his fool mind. "What are we going to tell Joy

10

and Dontae? I mean…you're not giving me anything to go on. We've been married twenty-five years and all of a sudden you just want out?"

"Like I said before, Joy and Dontae will be fine." He picked up his suitcase again and said, "I'm done discussing this. I'll be back to get the rest of my clothes. You should receive the divorce papers in a day or two. Just sign them and put them on the kitchen table." He headed toward the front door.

Following behind him, Carmella began screaming, "I'm not signing any divorce papers, so don't waste your time sending them here. And when you get off of whatever drug you're on, you'll be grateful that I didn't sign."

After opening the front door, Nelson turned to face his wife. With anger in his eyes, he said, "You better sign those papers or you'll regret it." He then stepped out of the house and slammed the door.

Carmella opened the door and ran after her husband. "Why are you doing this, Nelson? How am I supposed to pay the house note or our other bills if you leave me like this?"

"Get back in the house. You're making a scene."

"You spring this divorce on me without a second thought about my feelings, but you have the nerve to worry about the neighbors overhearing us?" Carmella shook her head in disgust. "I knew you were selfish, Nelson. But I never thought you were heartless."

He opened his car door and got in. "You're not going to make me feel guilty about this, Carmella. It's over between us. I want a divorce."

As Nelson backed out of the driveway, Carmella put her hands on her hips and shouted, "Well, you're not getting one!"

She stood barefoot, hands on hips, as Nelson turned what had seemed like an ordinary day into something awful and hideous. He backed out of the driveway—and out of her life—if what he said was to be believed. Carmella had been caught off guard...taken by surprise by this whole thing. Nelson had always been a family-values, family-first kind of man. He loved his children, and she'd thought he loved her as well. The family had attended church together and loved the Lord. But in the last year, Nelson had found one reason after another for not attending Sunday services.

"Are you okay?"

Carmella had been in a daze, watching Nelson drive out of her life; so she hadn't noticed that Cynthia Drake, their elderly next-door neighbor was outside doing her weekly gardening. Carmella wiped the tears from her face and turned toward the older woman.

"Is there anything I can do?" Cynthia asked, as she took off her gardening gloves.

"W-what just happened?" Carmella asked with confusion in her eyes.

"Come on," Cynthia said. She grabbed hold of Carmella's arm. "Let me get you back in the house."

"Why is everybody so obsessed with this house? It's empty, nobody in it but me. What am I supposed to do here alone?"

Cynthia guided Carmella back into the house and sat her down on the couch. "I'm going to get you something to drink." She disappeared into the kitchen and came back with a glass of iced tea and a can of Sunkist orange soda. "I didn't know which one you might want."

Carmella reached for the soda. "The iced tea is Nelson's. I don't drink it."

Cynthia sat down next to Carmella. She put her hand on Carmella's shoulder. "Do you want to talk?"

"Talk about what?" Carmella opened the Sunkist and took a sip. "I don't even know what's going on. I mean... I thought we were happy. I had no idea that Nelson wanted a divorce, but evidently, he's been planning this for a while."

"You need to get a divorce lawyer," Cynthia said.

"I don't want a divorce. I don't know what has gotten into Nelson, but he'll be back."

"You and Nelson have been married a long time, so I hope you're right. It would be a shame for him to throw away his marriage after all these years."

Carmella put the Sunkist down, put her head in her hands and started crying. This was too much for her. Nelson was the father of her children. He was supposed to love her for the rest of her life. They had stood before God and vowed to be there for each other, through the good and the bad, until death. How could he do this to her?

"Here, hon. Dry your face." Cynthia handed Carmella some tissue. "Do you have any family members that I could call to have them come sit with you for a while?"

"My parents have been dead for years and my only brother died last week," she said miserably.

"Oh hon, I'm so sorry to hear that."

Carmella lifted her hands and then let them flap back into her lap. "I just don't understand. I thought we were happy."

Sitting down next to Carmella, Cynthia said, "I've been married three times, and honey, trust me when I tell you that you'll probably never understand. Men don't need a reason for the things they do."

They sat talking for a while, and Carmella was comforted by the wise old woman who had taken time out from her gardening to sit with her in her time of need. When Cynthia was ready to leave, Carmella felt as if she should do something for the kindly old woman. She ran to the kitchen and came back with the sweet potato soufflé that she had lovingly fixed for her husband. She handed it to Cynthia, and said, "Thank you. I don't know what I would have done if you hadn't helped me back into the house."

"Oh, sweetie, it was no problem. You don't have to give me anything."

"I want to. I made this sweet potato soufflé for my husband. But since he doesn't want it, it would bring me great joy knowing that another family enjoyed it."

"Well, then I'll take it."

After Carmella walked Cynthia out, she went to the upstairs bathroom. She lit her bathroom candles, turned on the hot water and then poured some peach scented bubble bath in the water. She got into the tub, hoping to soak her weary bones until the ache in her heart drifted away. The warm water normally soothed her and took her mind off the things that didn't get done that day or the things that didn't turn out just the way she'd planned. Carmella enjoyed the swept-away feeling she experienced when surrounded by bubbles and her vanilla-scented candles. But tonight, all she felt was dread. She wondered if anyone would care if she drifted off to sleep, slid down all the way into the water and drowned like Whitney Houston had done.

The thought was tempting, because Carmella didn't know if she wanted to live without her husband. Tears rolled down her face as she realized that as much as she didn't want to live without Nelson, he was already living without her.

Two

"You better be glad we're friends, Jasmine. Because I would have to charge you for making me carry this heavy headboard if we weren't," Joy Marshall said. She put the headboard down and massaged her arm.

Jasmine Walker grinned. "You know I appreciate you, girl."

"Well, I would appreciate this mystery man of yours, if he showed up to do the heavy lifting."

Jasmine poked her bottom lip out. "He's at work, Joy. Come on, help me load this stuff on the truck, and I promise I'll make him take everything off the truck."

They picked up the headboard and made their way to the truck. "So, I'm finally going to meet this mystery man who swept you off your feet, but never bothered to pick you up for dates." Joy rolled her eyes. "I truly don't understand why you've kept on seeing him. For as long as I've known you, you've never let a guy treat you so cavalierly."

They placed the headboard in the truck, and then Jasmine said, "Well, he's made up for it now, hasn't he?"

"I don't know, Jasmine... renting is temporary. If he were really serious, he would have bought the house and bought a ring."

Jasmine put her arm around Joy's shoulder as they walked back into the house to get the rest of her things. "You'll see, Joy Marshall, my man loves me, and he's going to prove it to the world."

Joy didn't respond. Jasmine had been secretive ever since she started seeing this mystery guy. In her gut, Joy knew the man was married. That had to be the reason Jasmine was sneaking around all the time. Joy's parents were Christians. They had done their best to instill good moral values in their children, so Joy couldn't condone what her friend was doing. But she and Jasmine had been friends since they'd been assigned as roommates during their freshman year of college. After graduating college, they'd both decided to attend law school.

Since Joy was a child, she'd dreamed of the day she would finish law school and then work in her father's law practice. Her father had changed the plans a bit when he became a judge, so now Joy and Jasmine planned to become partners in their own law firm. Their plan included five years of clerking or doing the grunt work at a respected law firm so that they could learn the ropes and network. The Honorable Nelson Marshall had given her plan two-thumbs up, so Joy knew that she and Jasmine were on the right track.

"I hope this guy you're moving in with understands that you and I are going to be business partners, and that we will need to stay in touch with each other."

"Oh, he knows. And believe me, he understands about business, so he won't get in our way."

It seemed strange to Joy that she and Jasmine never said her boyfriend's name. The one time that Joy had demanded that Jasmine tell her who she was going out with, just in case the guy was a serial killer or something, Jasmine had claimed that his name was Charles Riley. But Joy didn't believe that. The name had sounded fake to her, and anyway, if his name were Charles, Jasmine would have referred to it every once in a while. But she had kept him strictly in the second-person category. The lawyer in Joy understood that Jasmine was trying not to slip up and say something she wasn't supposed to, but what?

After they'd packed all of Jasmine's bedroom furniture in the U-Haul truck, Jasmine jumped behind the wheel and Joy got in on the passenger's side. As they drove down the highway toward Jasmine's new home, Joy said, "Troy and I would like to take you and your man out to dinner next week. Do you think he would be willing to go somewhere with your friends?"

"You act like I'm moving in with Shrek. I promise you, Joy, my man is not an ogre."

"That's good to know, girl. I just want you to be happy," Joy said, and then leaned back in her seat.

"I am," Jasmine said. She exited off the highway. "He makes me so happy... I honestly can't believe that he chose me. I really think you'll be happy for us once you see how good we are together."

Joy hoped that Jasmine was right. She had worried about her friend getting too wrapped up in a guy who wouldn't even pick her up for dates, but made Jasmine meet him, as if he were too busy to drive a few blocks out of his way. Joy wouldn't have been able to put up with a man like that. She thanked God every day that her fiancé, Troy, was just like her father: considerate, responsible and loving.

"We're here." Jasmine pulled the U-Haul truck into the driveway of a spacious two-story home.

Joy's eyes widened as she looked at the house. From the looks of the outer structure, Joy figured the house had to be at least four thousand square feet. "Are you sharing this place with another couple or something?"

Jasmine laughed. She then shook her head. "No, he likes to entertain, so we needed enough room to be able to host parties."

"You sound like my mother. She's always hosting one party or another for my dad. You need to go take some cooking lessons from her so you can really do your parties up right," Joy suggested.

"Girl, please, I don't plan to do any cooking. That's what caterers are for," Jasmine opened the truck door and got out. Joy opened her door and followed Jasmine into the house.

Standing in the foyer, Joy was once again struck by the expansiveness of the house. The white marble floors, spiral staircase and the upstairs balcony that overlooked the foyer—all gave the house a feel of importance, as if someone with stature and influence lived there. "How can your guy afford to rent a house like this?" She knew it was rude to ask, but the question was out of her mouth before she could stop herself.

"Girl, just help me get those boxes out of the truck and stop being so nosey," Jasmine said with a good-natured grin on her face.

"I just can't believe this place, Jasmine. Troy and I sure can't afford anything like this."

They headed back out to the truck. "Once the two of you put your money together," Jasmine said, "I'm sure you'll be able to afford something nice, so don't sweat it, Joy."

"Please. After we get married, we'll probably spend the next five to ten years paying off our student loans. After that, we'll be able to start saving for a house like this."

Jasmine pulled a box out of the back of the truck. "I'm trying not to think about my student loans. At least your parents paid most of your tuition. But what I didn't get in financial aid, I had to cover in student loans."

Joy grabbed a box, and as they walked back to the house, she said, "Yeah, just when I started feeling grateful about not having so much debt to pay back after college, I met Troy and it seems like his middle name is debt."

"See, if you would have listened to me, you would have hooked up with an older guy who'd already paid off his debt. That way he would be able to take care of you in style."

They set the boxes down in the foyer and as they turned to go get more, Joy said, "I'm happy with Troy. Besides, my father had a lot of school debt when he married my mom, but they worked together and paid everything off. They're living pretty well now."

Jasmine didn't respond. She grabbed the next box and took it into the house. They followed that same process until all the boxes were unloaded.

Exhausted, they sat down on the floor next to the boxes. Joy said, "I don't think I want to be your friend anymore."

"I understand. I'm so tired; I don't want to move from this spot."

The two women sat on the floor, exhausted and breathing hard for a few minutes, and then Jasmine said, "You're right, he should have helped me move this stuff. But don't worry; I'm going to make him pay for our labor."

"Now you're talking like the Jasmine I know." Joy rubbed her hands together in sweet anticipation. "I wish I could be a fly on the wall when he gets what's coming to him."

Jasmine stood up. She held out her hand to help Joy up. "Come on," Jasmine said. "Let's order a pizza and watch Lifetime. I'll get my mystery man to take you home when he gets here."

"That's the least he can do," Joy said, as she stood up and headed toward the family room with Jasmine.

After Jasmine called the pizza in, they sat down and started watching a stalker movie on Lifetime. Halfway through it, the doorbell rang. Jasmine and Joy looked at each other; neither wanted to move now that they had found a comfortable spot on the sofa.

Jasmine finally got up. "All right," she said. "It's my house, so I've got to start doing the work around here."

When Jasmine came back with the pizza, Joy grabbed a slice and then leaned back against the sofa again. She took a bite. "This is good."

Jasmine savored the ham, sausage, pepperoni and cheese. She swallowed and agreed, "Sure is. It tastes just like that three-meat pizza we used to order during freshman year."

"You mean it tastes like the three-meat pizza I used to order. And you and our other roommate used to beg me for a slice."

As soon as the words were out of her mouth, Joy wanted to take them back. Jasmine hated when anyone referred to how impoverished she had been during their first few years of college. Things were going pretty well for her now, so Joy thought she had gotten over her issues with growing up in a single-parent household, with food stamps and government cheese. But the look of embarrassment that she saw in her friend's eyes made Joy want to put the pizza down and eat her words instead.

"I'm sorry, Jasmine; I didn't mean to upset you."

Jasmine waved off Joy's apology. "Stephanie and I made our way through college on scholarships, financial aid, and work programs that helped pay for those expensive books. We didn't always have extra money for pizza."

Joy grabbed another slice and lifted it in the air in a toast, and then said, "But you do now."

"Oh, I intend to have a lot more than pizza money, believe that," Jasmine said with a self-assured grin on her face.

"I have no doubt. I've always believed that you would succeed. I certainly wouldn't be thinking about starting a law firm with someone I thought didn't know what they were doing."

"I forgot to get something to drink. We have lemonade and iced tea in the fridge."

"I'll take the lemonade."

Jasmine stood. "I'll be right back. Do you need anything else?"

"A pillow. I'm about to crash." Joy pulled out her cell phone. "I'm going to have Troy come pick me up. Your man is taking too long."

"Suit yourself, but he should be here any minute." As if on cue, the doorbell rang. "Can you get that for me, Joy? I'm going to go get our drinks."

"Sure," Joy said. She got up and headed toward the front door. Before she could get to it, the doorbell rang again, and then the person on the outside started pounding on the door. Joy was walking as fast as she could, so whoever was so anxious would have to wait. She was too tired to move any faster.

By the time she got to the door, the doorbell rang for the third time. Joy was tempted to stand there a little longer and let the person on the other side of the door suffer a while longer. But when she looked through the peephole and saw her father, she immediately swung the door open.

As Nelson Marshall stepped into the house, he said, "I lost my key again."

Joy didn't hear him because as he was talking, she asked, "What are you doing here, Dad? Did Mom send you after me or something?"

Nelson swung around to face his daughter. His eyes widened. He stuttered, "Wh-what are y-you doing h-here?"

"I'm helping Jasmine move into her new house," Joy told her father. Then with a look of confusion on her face, she asked, "If you didn't know I was here, why did you come to Jasmine's house?"

Before Nelson could respond, Jasmine walked into the room carrying two glasses of lemonade. She handed one to Joy and then walked over to Nelson, kissed him, and then handed him the other glass. "You're late. What took you so long to get home?"

Nelson stepped back and turned toward his daughter. "I-I can explain."

But Joy was figuring things out all on her own. Jasmine's mystery man was her father, and the two of them had been sneaking around for over a year. "The person you need to explain something to is my mother," Joy declared, storming into the family room and grabbing her purse.

This was too much for Joy. Her father wasn't a cheater. He was a good man who went to work every day and attended church on Sundays with his family. But as she walked back into the entryway and saw the smirk on Jasmine's face, Joy began to believe what her eyes were telling her.

"You did this on purpose," Joy accused Jasmine. "You wanted me to know that my father was cheating on my mother."

Jasmine put her arm around Nelson and said, "It's time you knew the truth."

Nelson stepped away from Jasmine again. "This isn't how I wanted to tell her, Jasmine. You had no right bringing Joy here without letting me know."

Tearfully, Joy said, "What are you doing, Dad? This is going to break Mother's heart."

Nelson tried to put his arm around Joy. She pulled away. "Your mother already knows that I want a divorce. I'm surprised she didn't tell you."

Joy asked, "Why didn't you tell me? I spoke to you last night, but I don't recall you saying anything about divorcing my mother, so you could move in with someone young enough to be your daughter."

"I'm a grown woman," Jasmine said, "and Nelson and I are happy, despite our age difference."

Joy turned her back to Jasmine and held up her hand. "Don't speak to me ever again. I am not interested in anything you have to say." With that, Joy headed for the door.

"Don't go like this, baby-girl," her father said. "I really want to help you understand why I decided to leave your mother."

Joy opened the door and then shot back at her father, "Oh, I know exactly what was on your mind." She walked through the door and slammed it behind her. Joy was so angry that she wanted to hit something. She had looked up to her father almost to the point of worship for as long as she could remember. Nelson Marshall had been a man of integrity... someone she, her brother and her mother could count on.

Tears rolled down Joy's face as she walked away from her father's new home. She heard the door open behind her, but didn't stop or turn around to see who was coming after her. She wanted nothing to do with her so-called best friend or her dishonorable father.

"Baby-girl, wait! Jasmine said that you need a ride home. Don't walk off like this."

She kept walking.

Nelson caught up with his daughter and grabbed her arm. "Let me explain."

"Get away from me."

"Don't act like a child, Joy. You know how life works."

Joy wiped the tears from her eyes as she swung around to face her father. "I sure do know how life works. Men who claim to love their wives turn around and cheat on them every day. But I never expected you to be one of those men." She was disgusted by her father. At that moment she was ashamed to call this man her father and the tears flowed again.

"Don't cry, baby-girl. Come on, let me take you home."

Joy backed away from her father. "No, I don't need you to take me home. You need to go home to your wife."

"I can't do that."

"Then leave me alone."

"I can't just leave you out here like this, Joy. I'm your father. It's my job to protect you."

She laughed at that. The man standing in front of her had just destroyed her belief in humanity, but he was talking about protecting her. "I'll call Troy. He can come get me."

She pulled her cell phone out of her purse and dialed her fiancé. When he answered, she explained that she needed a ride, and Troy promised to come and pick her up. She hung up the phone and turned back to her father. "There, I don't need you, so you can go back to your little girlfriend and continue tearing our family apart."

Three

In the kitchen with her radio tuned to 92.7, her praise station, Carmella was busy baking cakes for her neighbors. Her way of saying thanks for the things they'd done for her in the past month: like mowing the law, trimming the bushes, coming by to check on her and just being kind to her. Dontae was still away at football camp, but would be home in two days. So, this was Carmella's way of letting her neighbors know that she appreciated them.

Cooking was a love of Carmella's; she could get in her kitchen and lose herself amongst the pots and pans and flour and sugar. She also loved listening to her praise music while she cooked or baked. Smokie Norful was lifting her spirit by telling her that God saw what was going on in her life and He understood when she felt like giving up. Then Smokie began encouraging her to keep moving forward, one more day, one more step.

Carmella was feeling it and was about to break out into a praise dance right in her kitchen, but then Joy walked in and killed the mood.

"Mama, why didn't you tell me that Daddy left you?"

Carmella had hoped not to have that discussion at all. She had prayed that Nelson would come to his senses and move back home where he belonged, before the children found out about his mid-life crisis. She'd thought he'd get the message when she didn't sign the divorce papers, but mailed the shredded document back to him. But Nelson had just sent her the document again. "Joy, this doesn't mean anything. Your Dad is just going through a mid-life crisis. He'll be back home soon enough."

Joy's eyebrow went up and she sat down at one of the counter seats. "You'd take him back after he moved Jasmine into his new house?"

Carmella took two lemon pound cakes out of the oven, closed the oven door with her foot and placed the cakes on her prep table. "What did you say, dear?"

Joy got up, walked further into the kitchen and stood next to her mother as she looked her in the face and said, "Daddy is living with my best friend, Jasmine."

She dumped the cakes out of the baking pans. "Don't say things like that, Joy. Where in the world would you get an idea like that?"

Joy put her hand on her mother's shoulder. "Listen to me, Mother. It's true. I saw it with my own eyes."

"Your father wouldn't do anything like that to us. He's a God-fearing man and he loves us." Carmella hadn't been feeling much love from her husband lately, but she didn't want to discuss any of that with Joy. Her daughter was a daddy's girl through and through. She hadn't even wanted Carmella to tuck her in at night when she was a child. Joy always asked for Nelson, to the point of hurting Carmella's feelings at times.

"Mom, come sit down with me in the family room." They walked out of the kitchen and made their way to the family room. Joy waited until her mother sat down on the sectional. Joy sat next to her and took her mom's hand in hers. "I helped Jasmine move today. She told me that her boyfriend had gotten a place for them. By the time we finished with moving things around in the house, Daddy showed up. I thought you had sent him to get me because I was taking too long, since I had called and told you that I would be coming over for dinner. But that wasn't why he was there."

Carmella was silent as she listened to her daughter. This doesn't seem like my life, she thought. Certainly doesn't sound like my husband, the man I married and promised to spend the rest of my life with. Nelson had been so sure that he would become a success in life and Carmella had just been grateful that he'd wanted her to be a part of what he was destined to create. They had spent a lot of nights praying for Nelson's career, his judgment and their finances. And just as Nelson had expected, their life had turned out great, with all the trimmings: a beautiful home, exotic vacations, college and mutual funds, the works.

"Dad admitted it to me, Mom. He said that you two were getting a divorce and that he was now with Jasmine."

"But that doesn't sound like Nelson," was all Carmella could fix her mouth to say. And then she thought, maybe it wasn't Nelson. Maybe some demon had come out of the pits of hell and climbed into her husband's body and was doing the slimy things that Nelson Marshall never would have dreamed of doing, if he wasn't under demonic possession.

"Mom... Mom. Where did you go?"

Joy was waving her hands in Carmella's face. "I'm still with you, Joy. I was just wondering if we should find a priest to perform an exorcism on your father or something." She then lowered her head and laughed hysterically.

"Mom, this isn't funny. Stop laughing."

But Carmella couldn't stop. Her husband had left her for a twenty-three-year-old recent college graduate, whom she'd fed numerous times in her own kitchen. If she didn't laugh, she'd cry until she drowned in her tears.

"I'm going to call Aunt Rose," Joy said as she jumped up and ran for the phone.

Rose had been Carmella's best friend since they roomed together in college. The two women had both married the year after graduating college. Their kids were born around the same time. They celebrated holidays and vacationed together. But even with all that, Carmella still hadn't called Rose to tell her that Nelson just up and walked out the door.

Rose made it to the house within fifteen minutes. The three women went into the kitchen. Carmella turned off the praise music and Joy and Rose helped her put icing on the cakes. "I need to get these to my neighbors. They have been so wonderful this past month and I want to show my appreciation."

"Hon, why didn't you call me? Why are you going through this alone?" Rose asked as she put the cream cheese frosting on one of the cakes. "And when did you have time to bake all of these cakes? There has to be at least twenty on the table."

"I have nothing but time," Carmella told her friend. "My husband no longer comes home and Dontae is still away at camp." She pointed towards Joy with a butter cream filled knife. "Joy has been staying in an apartment with Nelson's girlfriend down by the college."

After saying that, Carmella put her knife down and then punched a hole in the cake she just frosted. "Can you believe such a thing? My husband has a girlfriend."

Rose came around the table and pulled Carmella into a hug. As they pulled apart, Rose said, "Why don't we just go kill him?"

"Hey, I may not like him very much, but he is still my father," Joy said as she objected to where the conversation was going.

"You just put frosting on that cake and let me talk to Rose." Carmella threw a warning look in her oldest child's direction and then turned back to Rose. "Since Nelson is the father of my children, do you think we could just put him in the hospital?"

"Mom!"

"Hey, she wanted to kill him." Carmella pointed at Rose.

Rose pointed towards the cakes, giggling so hard, she could barely get a word out. When she finally collected herself she said, "Remember that movie, The Help?" she asked and then doubled over with laughter.

"Yeah, I remember The Help. You and I went to see it together. I'm still mad about that outhouse mess."

"Speaking of mess…" Rose said as she came up for air.

"Aunt Rose, I know you aren't suggesting that my saint of a mother bake a cake full of poo for my dad?"

Carmella put her hand over her mouth and her eyes widened as she began to understand what her friend was trying to tell her. "Rose, you are crazy, girl."

"What? You said you wanted to put him in the hospital. Don't you think eating a dung filled cake would do it?"

"Girl, I have too much respect for cakes to treat one so harshly."

"Well you're the one who wanted to put him in the hospital," Rose reminded her.

"By running him over or something like that, not by ruining one of my beautiful cakes."

Joy stepped away from the prep table. "I'm going to my room." As she walked out of the kitchen, she threw back, "And I hope I won't be testifying against my mother any time soon."

Carmella and Rose laughed, then Carmella got serious and said, "She's right. The man is my husband. I've been married to him for twenty-five years. I shouldn't be talking like this."

"He asked you for a divorce, Carmella. It's time to fight, girl. Do something," Rose told her as she bounced around the kitchen as if she were getting ready for a boxing match.

"I don't know how to fight," Carmella confessed. "All I've ever done is be Nelson's obedient pup, run his errands and take care of his house. I haven't even put the degree I worked so hard to get to use in over twenty years."

Carmella sat down on one of the stools in the kitchen, laid her head on the counter and cried like tears were rain and she was doing her part to end an all consuming drought.

Another day, another problem. Two days ago she'd cried on Rose's shoulder and then went door to door passing out pound cakes to her neighbors. This morning she was awakened out of her fitful sleep by the ringing of the phone. Carmella had tried to ignore it and sleep on, but it seemed as if it would stop ringing for a moment and then start back up again. Somebody wanted to speak with her, and they weren't going to give up until she answered the phone.

With her head still on the pillow, Carmella reached over to her night stand and took the phone off the hook. She put the receiver against her ear and mumbled, "Hello."

"Hi, may I speak with Mr. or Mrs. Marshall."

Her voice was groggy as she responded, "This is Mrs. Marshall. Who's calling?"

"This is Rita from Wells Fargo. We're just giving you a friendly reminder call concerning your mortgage."

That woke Carmella. She popped up in bed and asked, "What about my mortgage? What's wrong?" She'd never received a call from her mortgage company before; why on earth were they calling her so early in the morning?

"We haven't received the payment this month and we just wanted to remind you that it was due on the first."

The first was two weeks ago. They were almost halfway through August. Had Nelson been so busy playing with his girl-child that he'd forgotten his responsibilities?

"I'll check into this and get back with you." Carmella hung up the phone.

A hot flash was overtaking her body, reminding her that she was forty-seven and pre-menopausal. She fanned herself with her hand, but that didn't help, so she opened the window and then realized it was August and hot as Hades outside. So she put the window down and turned the ceiling fan on. Just as she was cooling off, the phone rang again.

Carmella picked it up, but didn't say anything. A recording asked her to wait for a very important message. The message was about the payment on her Lexus SRX 400 being past due. "Oh, I know he done fell and bumped his head now."

She dialed Nelson's office, not caring that he would need to be on the bench within fifteen minutes and was probably handling some last minute judgeship stuff. She needed to speak with her husband and nobody was going to stop her. So when Laura, his long time secretary answered the phone, Carmella said, "Good morning, Laura, I hope your morning is going well."

"It is, Mrs. Marshall."

She noticed that Laura didn't ask how her morning was going. No doubt Laura already knew about Nelson's mistress. So she was probably worried that Carmella would break down on her and tell her all sorts of horrid things about her boss. "Listen Laura, I need to speak with my husband. I know he's probably busy, but I don't care about his schedule right now. I'm having a crisis and I need him on the phone ASAP."

"I'll put you through this instant, Mrs. Marshall." Just before transferring the call, Laura mumbled, "I'm sorry."

Carmella heard her and appreciated that she would let her feelings be known in the slightest way. But when Nelson picked up, she had no time to dwell on that kindness. "Why haven't you paid the mortgage or my car note?" she screamed at him.

"Good morning to you, too, Carmella. How are things going?" he asked in a calm manner as if everything was right with the world and the sun was shining down on him alone.

"I was awakened by bill collectors this morning, Nelson, so I'm not having a good morning. But I bet your little girlfriend was able to sleep soundly this morning."

"Jasmine doesn't sleep in like you. She has a job to get to every morning."

Carmella was livid. She had worked her fingers to the bone, making a home for her family and being the perfect hostess for Nelson. "How can you be so cruel as to disparage the work I've done for this family? Being a housewife is no longer good enough for you, I guess."

"No one is belittling what you did for our family. But don't you think it's time to get a job and handle your own bills?"

"No, I do not!" You're the one who left this family. And we have depended on your income for over twenty years now, right after you stopped depending on my income to get you through law school. And I guarantee you that any judge in this town would agree with me." She was out of her bed pacing the floor. "You are not going to get away with this, Nelson Marshall. If you want to live a double life, then you darn well better find the money to pay for both of them."

"Sign the divorce papers and then I'll make sure you get a decent settlement."

"In your dreams," she said and slammed down the phone. She was just about to throw it against the wall, when her bedroom door opened and Joy and Dontae rushed in. She'd totally forgotten that Joy was picking Dontae up from the airport this morning. Had he heard her? Oh God, she prayed not.

"Mom, why are you in here screaming about Dad living a double life? What's going on?"

Prayer wasn't doing her a bit of good lately. She fell back onto her bed and began screaming and crying—anything to avoid answering Dontae's question.

"Come on, Dontae; let me talk to you in the other room," Joy said as she watched her mother fall apart."

"B-but, what's wrong with Mom?" He went to his mother and tried to calm her. "Did I upset you, Mama? If I did, I didn't mean to, so please stop crying."

"It's not you, baby," was all she could say before the tears came again.

Joy pulled Dontae out of the bedroom and then Carmella sat up in the middle of the bed. She grabbed one of the fluffy pillows on Nelson's side of the bed and held it close to her chest, while resting her face in it. The pillow still smelled of his cologne. Carmella inhaled deeply. She'd always loved the way the Dolce & Gabbana pour Homme fragrance smelled on Nelson. It was woodsy and masculine. The fragrance was not for daytime wear because it could be a bit overpowering, so Nelson only wore it during evening events. When she stopped and thought about it, she realized that he had stepped out a lot of nights without her in the last few months.

She should have been more suspicious… paid more attention to what was going on right under her nose. She threw the pillow across the room, as the fragrance she used to love was now making her stomach curdle. She had been played for a fool and now she had to figure out how she was going to pay bills that Nelson had always assured her that she need not concern herself with.

She had graduated with a bachelor's degree in Art. But she never received her teaching certificate or attended graduate school so that she might be able to teach art in elementary or even at a community college. She'd married Nelson six months after graduation and then she'd had to work temp assignments and receptionist positions so she could bring money into the home while Nelson went on to law school. Once he'd finished school, she'd had their first child and he'd asked her to stay home and raise their children.

Funny thing was, Carmella had always thought she'd gotten the long end of the stick. While Nelson was forced to go out and work for a living and deal with the rat race, she had been able to stay home with her children and concentrate on keeping her home happy. But now that she was unemployable in this new economy, it hurt like a son of gun to realize that she'd actually gotten the short and frayed end of that stick.

Four

"He did what?" Dontae exploded. "How come no one called to tell me any of this? Why am I just now finding out that my father has been sleeping with your best friend for a year?"

"You think I knew any of this was going on?" Joy got defensive.

"Well, she is your best friend. And you did let her live with you."

"She was a roommate. And we are no longer best anything. The woman used me the whole time and threw her relationship with Daddy in my face." Joy plopped down on the sofa and began crying.

Dontae went to his sister, put his arm on her shoulder and said, "I didn't mean that. I know it's not your fault."

"I just can't believe any of this is happening. Daddy and Mommy always seemed so happy. They went to church together for goodness' sake." Joy was simply outdone over the things that had transpired over the last few days. Her father's betrayal had shaken her core beliefs and she was now having second, third, fourth and fifth thoughts about her upcoming wedding. On paper Troy was a good man...a good catch. But would that paper be tarnished twenty years from now?

"We've got to do something. We can't just sit here and let Daddy get away with this. I've never seen Mama cry like that."

"I know Dontae, but what can we do?"

"Let's go talk to Daddy," Dontae suggested.

Joy folded her arms around her chest. "I don't have anything to say to that man."

"Well I've got a lot I want to say, so if you're not going, I'll just drive myself." Dontae grabbed the keys to the three year old Mustang his father bought him on his sixteenth birthday and headed out the door.

Joy went into the kitchen, spread some vegetable cream cheese on a wheat bagel, poured orange juice into a glass and grabbed a banana. She then took the light breakfast to her mother's room. As she placed the plate on the night stand, she told her mother, "I'm leaving for class, but I need to make sure that you're going to be all right."

Carmella struggled to lift her head from her pillow and then flopped back down. "I'm just tired, Joy."

"I know you're tired, Mother. And I understand. But I don't want you getting sick over this."

"Let me lay here for a little while longer and then I promise I'll get up and eat something." Carmella closed her eyes and appeared to shrink back into her bed.

Joy couldn't bear to see her mother like that. And knowing that her father caused the pain was crushing. She didn't want to see him, which was a problem, because she worked for her father. Three days a week after school, Joy made her way to Judge Nelson Marshall's office to clerk for him. Her father wanted her to see what working lawyers did all day as they came in and out of the courthouse. Joy was in her last year of law school, with only two more classes to go before graduation. But at that point, she was so confused that she didn't know what to do.

She had picked her major because her father had been an excellent lawyer and was now an incredible judge. But the fact that he turned out to be such a lousy husband outweighed it all. So, even though she went to class like a good little law student, she absorbed absolutely nothing of what had been taught that day. Instead of going to work, she went back to the apartment that she had all to herself and typed up a resignation letter for her father, the judge.

She then walked around the elegant, two bedroom apartment that had been her home for the last two years and simply waved goodbye to the rooms. She had enough sense to realize that every action deserved a reaction. She was going to quit her job, so her father wasn't going to be in the mood to continue paying her rent. And besides, he now had a girlfriend and a wife to take care of, so the twenty-three-year-old daughter would just have to fend for herself.

Her cell phone rang. She sat down on her sofa and pulled the phone out of her Gucci bag, saw that it was Troy calling and answered, "Hey babe."

"Hey yourself. I was just calling to check on you. I haven't heard from you in a couple of days and just wanted to make sure everything was all right."

She kept meaning to return his calls, but then something else in her suddenly dysfunctional family life would happen. "I'm sorry. I haven't been ignoring your calls, it's just that my mother is really having a tough time dealing with what my father has done and I've been spending my time with her."

"I understand that." Troy paused and then asked, "Have you talked to your father?"

"No, and I don't plan to either," Joy quickly remarked.

"Joy, I don't want you to get upset with me, but he is still your father. You can't ignore him forever."

She rolled her eyes. Men... they were all in cahoots together. Joy was quickly learning that you couldn't trust them. Who knew what Troy was doing behind her back? And then she wondered just what type of behavior Troy would expect his children to accept from him. "So, I guess once we have children and you do me dirty, you think they should just continue giving Daddy a hug and kiss, never mind what you did to their mother."

"Joy, where is this coming from? I don't have plans on doing you wrong. Our children will never have to decide between their mother and father, because they will always have both of us."

She harrumphed. "That's what you say now. But just let me have two or three children, and gain a few pounds, then we'll see about that wandering eye of yours."

"What wandering eye?" Troy sighed. "Look Joy, I can see that you're going through a difficult time. But I need you to understand that I am not your father. My name is Troy Anderson and I love you."

She didn't respond. She wanted to, but for the life of her, Joy couldn't fathom the appropriate response. Love seemed like this empty word people loosely threw around. Because what did love really mean anyway? It certainly didn't mean that the person would stay with you through sickness and whatever else came your way.

"I'll talk to you later, Joy. Just give me a call when you feel like talking, okay?"

"All right, Troy. Thanks for calling," she said as if responding to a caller who had just given condolences for the death of a family member.

She put her cell phone back in her purse, stood, and got ready to leave her apartment when the house phone rang. She rarely received calls on that line. Only family and Troy and Jasmine knew the number. She stepped over to the phone and recognized the number as one that was coming from the county court system. But it wasn't any of the numbers associated with her father's office so, being curious, she picked it up.

As she said, "Hello," Joy was informed that she had a collect call from Dontae. *What in the world is that boy doing calling me collect? Couldn't he have gone back over to Daddy's office and made the call rather than using one of the pay phones?* She accepted the call and then asked, "Boy, don't be calling me collect. I am a poor college student and I can no longer afford such luxuries."

"Sis, I need your help. I'm in jail."

"You're where?" She was shouting, but she couldn't help it. The last thing she ever expected her studious and athletic brother to call and say to her was that he was in jail. *Lord, help them all.* "What happened?"

"I don't want to talk about it. Just come and get me, okay? I don't want to spend the night in this place. They say I can be bonded out for five hundred dollars."

She loved her brother, but she had just spent all of her money on her annual end of summer shopping spree and didn't have five hundred dollars to her name, or on either one of her credit cards. "I'll get you out, Dontae. I'll be there as soon as I get my hands on the money; don't you worry."

The minute she hung up with Dontae, she picked the phone back up to call her mother. But then she thought better of that. Her mother was already dealing with so much that Joy didn't want to bother her with this. She dreaded what she was about to do, but she had no other choice than to call her father.

When he picked up the phone he said, "There you are. I was wondering why you didn't come to work today."

She didn't respond to that, instead she said, "Daddy, Dontae is in jail and I need five hundred dollars to get him out."

"I know where Dontae is," he said calmly.

"Oh, so have you already paid his bail?"

"No, and I don't intend to. He can spend the night in that cell and think about what he did," Nelson responded.

"Excuse me?"

"That brother of yours came to see me this morning. I took him to lunch and then gave him the address to my new house and asked him to come by this evening so we could talk some more." Nelson let out a frustrated sigh before he continued. "Instead of waiting until I got off work, Dontae went to the house and threw rocks through the window. He even busted out the windshield on Jasmine's car."

"Okay, but why did you call the police on him?" Joy asked, her temperature rising by the second.

"I didn't call the police on him. Jasmine did. But I was in total agreement with her. No son of mine is going to get away with acting like that."

"Oh, so you have no mercy for Dontae, but you think your actions deserve a get-out-of- jail-free card?"

"What's that supposed to mean?" Nelson asked.

"Are you going to give me the money for Dontae or not?" She was done with their conversation.

"I told you. I'm going to do what's best for Dontae and let him sit and think about his actions."

Click. She slammed the phone down so hard, she hoped that her father's eardrum burst on impact. But people like Nelson Marshall never found themselves in harm's way. They just somehow always found ways to hurt others.

Joy hated disturbing her mother with something like this. But she had no other choice. She picked the phone back up and dialed her mother. The line was busy. Joy waited ten seconds and then dialed again... still busy.

She didn't have time to sit there and wait for somebody to help her. Joy left her apartment and raced to her mother's house. She dialed her number twice from her cell phone while en route, but the line stayed busy.

She pulled up to her mother's house and jumped out of the car. She unlocked the front door and rushed into the house. It was five in the evening. Her mother was normally in the kitchen, cooking up something good at that time of day, but she wasn't there. It didn't seem as if the kitchen had seen any activity the entire day. Joy left the kitchen and took the stairs two at a time, headed to the master bedroom.

Joy knocked on the door and then opened it. Her mother was snoring like a hibernating bear. She looked over at the nightstand and noticed that the phone was off the hook. Joy shook her head as she hollered, "Mama... wake up, Mama." She put the phone back on the hook.

Carmella jumped up and screamed, "No! Take the phone back off the hook, they won't stop calling."

"Who won't stop calling?"

"Bill collectors. They harassed me so bad this morning that I had to take a nerve pill."

Now her mother was on nerve pills. Thank you again, Judge Nelson Marshall. "You've got to get out of bed, Mama. Dontae vandalized Daddy's new house and now he's in jail."

"What? Who's in jail," Carmella asked, looking out of it and like she was ready to fall back to sleep.

Joy pulled the covers off of Carmella. "Stay with me, Mama. I need you to focus."

Carmella stretched, yawned and then swung her feet to the floor. "I'm focused. Now, what's going on?"

"Dontae is in jail. We have to bail him out."

"What? My baby is in jail?"

"Yes, so please put some clothes on so we can go pick him up. His bond is five hundred dollars, and I don't have it."

"I can get a cash advance on my Discover card." Carmella jumped up and went into her walk-in closet. She threw on a white tee-shirt and a pair of jeans. While she was putting on a pair of sandals, the phone rang. "Don't pick it up," she warned Joy.

"Mother, I've never known you to be afraid to answer your phone." She shook her head and picked up the phone. "Hello."

"May I speak with Mr. or Mrs. Marshall?"

Feeling ornery, Joy said, "Who is calling and what do you want?"

"I'm calling concerning a personal business matter. Is Mrs. Marshall in?"

"What is this personal business matter?" Joy demanded.

Carmella rushed out of her closet, took the phone away from Joy and hung it up. "Didn't I tell you not to answer?"

"Daddy stopped paying the bills?" Joy's mouth hung slack as she began to understand what was going on.

Carmella was embarrassed, but she shook her head, confessing that, "He won't pay anything until I sign the divorce papers."

"You need to clean him out," Joy said angrily. "Take every dime he has."

"One thing at a time, Joy Marshall." Carmella grabbed her purse. "I need you to drive me downtown so I can get your brother out of jail. When we get back, then we can work on ways to get the money out of your father."

Five

"I can't believe that girl had the nerve to have my son arrested after she stole my husband," Carmella said as they arrived back at her house with Dontae in tow.

"I'm sorry about getting arrested, Mama. But I'm not sorry about busting out their windows. They deserve that and more."

"Stop talking foolishness, Dontae. That arrest could destroy your chances for getting into Harvard."

"I don't even want to go to Harvard anymore, anyway. So, who cares," Dontae said as he sulked off.

"Another dream Nelson has stolen," Carmella said of her son no longer desiring to go to Harvard. She lifted her hands to heaven and turned toward the kitchen. "Let me get dinner started. At least we still have some food around here."

Joy sat down on the sofa and turned on the television.

Carmella opened the fridge and started pulling out mushrooms, onions, and garlic before even thinking about turning on her radio as she normally did whenever she walked into the kitchen. She pulled a stainless steel pot down and filled it with water. She placed it on the stove, turned on the fire and then turned around to grab the rest of her ingredients for the pasta dish she was about to fix. But that's when she noticed that the faucet was dripping again. She'd asked Nelson time and time again to fix that faucet and he'd ignored her just as he'd ignored everything else she'd asked him to do. Well, he wasn't getting away with it this time.

She pulled open one of the kitchen drawers and took a pair of pliers out, then grabbed her car keys and headed for the door.

Joy jumped up. "Where are you going?"

"To get your daddy," Carmella said, not breaking her stride.

"Whoa, whoa, whoa." Joy put herself between her mother and the front door. "You can't go over there. Jasmine already had Dontae arrested. What do you think she'll do to you?"

"I wish that twig would say something out the way to me. I'll break her scrawny little neck."

"That still sounds like jail time to me, Ma." Joy held onto the door. "I can't let you do this."

"Girl, get out of my way." Carmella's eyes were wild as she shoved Joy out of her way and bulldozed

53

through the door. Joy had told her where Nelson was staying the day she'd come home upset about his love nest. So now, she jumped in her car and raced over to the place where her husband's heart now resided. But she didn't care about any of that right then. What Carmella cared about was the fact that Nelson Marshall had stood before God and two hundred other folks and made promises to her. She now knew that Nelson wasn't an honorable man, but he was going to have to scrape up some honor that night or she was going upside his bald head.

As she stood in front of the house that her husband now shared with his mistress, she gagged as she tried to hold down vomit that threatened to spill over. She pressed her finger on the buzzer. When no one answered the door, she leaned on the buzzer. Someone looked out the blinds and then quickly closed them. "You might as well open the door," Carmella started screaming, not caring who heard her. "I want my husband out of this house right now."

When they still didn't open the door, she turned and started shouting towards the neighboring houses. "That's right, everybody. You've got an adultery-committing judge and his slimy teenaged slut living in this house right here." She pointed towards Nelson's house. "My husband's girlfriend used to come to my house with my daughter for evening and holiday meals. So if you women on this block know what's good for you, you'll watch your men, and you won't let this hussy in your house for sugar or a crust of bread." Carmella was jabbing a finger toward Nelson's door with every word.

The door opened and Nelson rushed out. "Now that's enough, Carmella."

She swung around to face him. "I just got started, so don't get in my way unless you want me to get in my car and run your no good, cheating behind over."

"Why are you doing this in front of our home?" Jasmine asked as she stepped out of the house but kept her distance from Carmella.

Carmella's arms were swinging wildly, the pliers in her hand almost connected with Nelson's jaw as she told Jasmine, "Oh, so you can come to my house and steal my husband, but I can't come over here and let the people know who they have in their neighborhood."

Jasmine's hand went to her hip. "Why do you think anyone would care that you can't keep a man?"

"Oh, I can keep a man. I kept him for twenty-five years, until you brought your man-stealing self to my house." Carmella pointed at her as she walked toward her. "You're just as bad as a pedophile. People ought to put your picture on their refrigerator and warn their men not to walk past this house."

"Shut up, Carmella. You're making a fool of yourself," Nelson screamed at her.

"Better I do it, than continue to let you do it," she told him as she swung back his way. She was just about in tears, but standing her ground.

"What do you want, Carmella?" Nelson asked as he turned and spotted the neighbors peeping through their windows and the ones who were bold enough, were just standing on their porches watching.

She handed him the pliers, and said in an almost begging tone, "I want you to come home so you can fix the faucet. It's dripping again."

Jasmine let out a great big belly laugh as she swung her long hair around and then said, "You're pathetic. No wonder Nelson doesn't want you anymore."

"Don't you talk to me!" Carmella screamed as she lunged at Jasmine.

The lady across the street yelled, "Get her! I've got a baseball bat over here if you really want to break her from stealing."

Carmella pulled Jasmine down to the ground and grabbed hold of her hair.

"That's right. Pull that weave out of her man-stealing head," another woman said as she stood on her porch, punching at the air as if she were in the fight against the woman who stole her man.

"Help me, Nelson," Jasmine screamed as she tried to defend herself against each blow that Carmella sent her way.

"Now C-Carmella, s-stop acting foolish." Nelson tried to pull his wife off of his mistress, but failed miserably. He then stepped around the side of the house and turned on the sprinklers.

Carmella felt the water and thought it was rain. The grip she had on Jasmine's hair slipped and Jasmine got up and ran back into the house. But Carmella stayed on the ground, punching and beating it if as she were still on top of Jasmine. She had no mercy as her hands continued to punish the ground beneath her.

"Get up, Carmella. Stop this," Nelson yelled.

Someone was talking behind her, but she couldn't make out what was being said. All she knew was that the rain was coming down and the dirt was flying all around her head. Suddenly, when the rain stopped, Carmella sat back, looked around as if she were lost and searching for something or someone.

Nelson was standing behind her. Cautiously, he asked, "Carmella, are you okay?"

"Did you fix the faucet?" she asked in a hollow, out-of-tune voice.

He inched toward her.

Carmella looked down at herself. The dirt and mud mingled with the soft fabric of her off white cashmere sweater. It was one of her favorite sweaters. She began screaming, "Why is all this dirt on me? Did you push me?" she yelled at Nelson as she got up and began chasing him around the yard with a crazed look in her eye. "How could you? How could you? You've dirtied my favorite sweater."

She lunged at him, but he stepped out of the way. "What's wrong with you, Carmella? You're acting crazy."

"I'm acting crazy?" She found a large stick in the yard and picked it up. "You ruin my best sweater... one I probably won't be able to replace, and then you claim I'm the crazy one?" She swung at him.

"Stop this and go home, Carmella. Someone is going to get hurt," he screamed as he cowered on the other side of his silver Mercedes.

"Looks like you're the one who's going to get hurt, you cheating dog," the woman from across the street yelled, enjoying the show.

Carmella swung the stick. "Why aren't you home?" she asked as the stick missed Nelson, but connected with the hood of his car.

Nelson yelped as if he had been hit, and attempted to rub the dent away. But when Carmella swung again, he had no choice but to bob and weave and let his car take whatever blows came its way.

Sirens were going off as Carmella swung from left to right at Nelson's head. But Carmella hadn't heard anything. She felt like one of those women on Snapped, because she wanted to draw blood and she didn't care whose blood it was. All she knew was that somebody had to pay for what had happened to her life.

Nelson fell back, Carmella then stood over him, paying no heed to the officers that approached. Carmella went somewhere inside of herself, hiding from all the pain that loving someone who didn't love her back brought. She lifted her arm for one more go at batting practice.

One police officer grabbed her arm. Carmella tried to jerk it back. She yelled at the officer to leave her alone and let her finish. "Nelson needed discipline."

The officer swung her to the ground. Carmella didn't even feel the impact. She laughed, and kept on laughing because her mind had taken her to a happy place... a place of peace. A place where she, Nelson and the kids frolicked on the sandy beach and Jasmine was nowhere in sight.

Six

Instead of being hauled off to jail for assault, the police officer decided to take Carmella to the hospital. Nelson had her placed on a seventy-two hour hold so she could be evaluated. But Carmella was in such hysterics when they brought her in that she had to be medicated. She was now despondent and only wanted to sleep... sleep her life away. Carmella had no idea how much time had passed since she'd first come to that place or what was happening to her. She was only slightly aware of the people that came in and out of her room. She couldn't focus. Carmella was powerless to do anything to help herself. So she woke in sadness, napped in sorrow and by night fall she had cried so much that she pretty much bathed in her own tears.

"I'm not going to just let you lay here and ignore us." Rose stood on the side of her friend's hospital bed with a take charge look on her face.

Someone was talking to her, but her head was so foggy she couldn't make out what was being said, or who was saying it.

Rose put her hand on Carmella's arm and shook her. "Snap out of it, girl. Nelson Marshall isn't worth all of this."

Nelson? Did somebody call for Nelson?

"What's wrong with her?" Dontae yelled.

"She's sad, Dontae. Haven't you seen how much she's been crying?" Joy asked, standing next to her brother.

"That's all she seems to do is cry. Why won't she talk to us?"

Rose shushed Dontae. "She can probably hear you, so watch what you say."

But Dontae wouldn't be silenced. He pointed towards his mother. "She's been lying like that for two days now. Why is she acting like this?"

"She doesn't feel well right now, Dontae, but she's going to get better. I promise you that," Rose assured him. She then turned to Joy and said, "Why don't you two go home and get some rest. I can hang out here with your mom for the rest of the day."

Joy put her arm around her brother as she said, "That's nice of you to offer, Aunt Rose. But she's our mother so I think we should be here with her."

"Have a seat, Dontae." Rose said as she grabbed Joy's hand and walked her out of the hospital room. They stood a few doors away from Carmella's room as Rose told Joy, "Listen to me, hon, your mom is going to get through this nightmare. But I don't think it's good for Dontae to see her like this."

"But what if something happens to her while we're gone?"

"Nothing's going to happen to Carmella. The doctors just have her over sedated, if you ask me. So the next thing I want you to do is to go to the nurse's station on your way out and demand that they hold off on giving Carmella any more medication until she climbs out of the fog they have her in."

Joy took a deep breath then nodded. "I can do that."

"Okay, now can you help me get Dontae out of here? And don't let him come back here until tomorrow."

Joy shook her head. "He won't agree to leave. He's too worried about Mama."

Rose grabbed hold of Joy's hand. "I promise you and your brother that even if I have to get on my knees and pray all night long, Carmella is going to be all right. Tomorrow is a new day. Dontae needs to see her then, but not now."

"Okay Aunt Rose, I think I have an idea to get Dontae out of here."

They went back into the room. Carmella was still lying motionless, with her face toward the wall. Dontae was seated with his head in his hands crying, the same way he'd cried when he was seven years old and his dog, Sam had died. Joy put her hand around his arm and pulled him up. "Come on Dontae, I need your help with something."

Joy headed towards the door, but Dontae stopped her. "We can't leave Mom. She needs us."

Joy shook her head. "Mom needs some rest right now. The best thing we can do is to allow her to rest without hearing us crying and talking back and forth over her head. Now, I've got some things I need to do at my apartment and you can help me with that."

Dontae looked back towards the bed.

"We'll be back in the morning to check on Mama," Joy assured him. "Now will you help me or not?"

He hesitated, then put his hands in his pockets and nodded as he walked through the door with his sister.

Joy peeked back in the room and told Rose, "Give her a kiss from me and Dontae and let her know that we'll be back in the morning."

"I'll do that," Rose said. Then as Joy closed the door behind her, Rose got on her knees and began petitioning God on her friend's behalf.

***

As Joy and Dontae headed out of the hospital, she made sure to stop by the nurse's station and requested that her mother not be given any more medication until she was alert enough to ask for it herself. She also explained to them that she was in law school and her father was a judge, so they knew how to file lawsuits if need be. She and Dontae then stopped by a local grocery store, grabbed a few empty boxes and then headed to her apartment.

"What are the boxes for?" Dontae asked.

"I'm moving out. I'll be staying with you and Mama for a little while."

Dontae's eyebrow went up as he questioned Joy, "Why would you do that? Dad pays your rent."

"In the back of my mind, I was kind of hoping that he would continue to pay my bills even though he's divorcing Mama. But after seeing her in the hospital like that, I don't want anything from that man."

"It's going to be pretty hard not taking anything from him since you work for him and he signs off on your paycheck."

She patted her purse and said, "Got my resignation letter right here. I will be mailing it off to him in the morning."

"You act like all of this is Dad's fault," Dontae said as they pulled up to Joy's apartment.

"Who else do you think I should blame? Mom didn't wreck our home; Dad did that all on his own." She got out of the car and grabbed a few of the flattened boxes.

Dontae grabbed the remaining boxes and followed her inside. As they were taping the boxes and placing them around the room, Dontae told his sister, "I blame Jasmine. She was always coming to our house acting all nice and innocent and all the while she was putting moves on our dad."

"Just remember, it takes two to tango."

Dontae threw a box to the opposite side of the room. "I know you're not defending that snake. It sounds like you still want to be friends with her, even after what she did to Mama."

"Stop throwing my boxes around. And no, I'm not defending Jasmine. And I certainly am not friends with her. I just think that Daddy should have known better. Jasmine obviously doesn't care who she hurts. But Daddy should have known that his actions would hurt the family." She stood up with two boxes in hand. "Let's box up as many of my clothes as possible and get them over to the house. I think I'm going to put my furniture on eBay, so I can earn a little money while I look for a job."

Dontae followed his sister around the apartment, doing as she instructed. After about two hours of boxing and moving things around so Joy could take pictures to post on eBay, they finally left the apartment and headed home.

As they pulled up to the house and noticed that their father's car was parked in the driveway, the brother and sister had two different thoughts.

"The nerve of him. He has no business being here," Joy said as she turned off the car.

"Maybe he's sorry for what he did and is ready to come back home," Dontae said as they got out of the car.

Joy rolled her eyes and ignored her brother. He was acting like a sap, wishing for something that simply wasn't going to happen. Because Joy knew in her heart that her father wasn't there looking for forgiveness. He was probably just trying to move more of his things out before their mom was released from the hospital. She stormed into the house, looking for a fight. Her father had been her hero. Now he was just the man who'd done them wrong. "What are you doing in here?" she asked, with hands on hips as she stepped into the kitchen and found her father tinkering with the faucet.

Nelson grabbed a towel and wiped his hands, then he closed the cabinets below the faucet. "Your mom asked me to fix the sink, so I came over to take care of it."

"Oh you're quite a prince, aren't you?" Joy said with an exasperated expression on her face.

Nelson's finger wagged in her face. "Now look here, young lady, you might not like what I've done, but I'm still your father and you will respect me."

Joy scoffed at that and folded her arms around her chest. "Respect you? Are you kidding? I don't even know who you are."

"Stop yelling at him, Joy. Dad's just trying to make things right again." Dontae turned to Nelson and asked, "Isn't that right, Dad?"

"Of course I want to make things right between us, son." Nelson turned to Joy and said, "I want to make things right with you, too, Joy Lynn."

Her father used to call her Joy Lynn when she was a little girl, when he had seemed like Superman to her.

Today she didn't want him to use her first name, let alone her middle name. "Is the sink fixed?"

"Yes, tell your mother that I took care of it." He shuffled his feet, looking uncomfortable in his own house.

Joy didn't say anything, just kept staring at her father with her arms folded and her lip twisted.

But Dontae piped up. "I'll let her know when we go back to the hospital in the morning, Dad."

"Thanks, son."

Joy rolled her eyes and shook her head. "Why are you sucking up to this man? He wouldn't even give me the money I needed to get you out of jail the other day... told me that you needed to spend the night in jail to teach you a lesson." Joy pointed an accusing finger at her father. "He's the reason Mama is in the hospital half out of her mind right now. If he would have given me the money, I wouldn't have even bothered Mama. She wouldn't have known that you had been arrested at all."

Dontae turned to his father. "Did you really tell Joy to leave me in that place?"

Seeing his one ally slipping away, Nelson hurriedly said, "I just wanted you to understand that there are consequences for actions, son. That's all."

"See what I've been trying to tell you, Dontae. This man—"

"Stop calling me, this man. I'm your father."

"Then you should act like it." Joy opened her purse and pulled out an envelope and handed it to her so-

67

called father. "I was going to mail this to you. But since you're here, I might as well hand it to you now."

"What is this?" Nelson asked.

"My resignation."

He tried to hand the envelope back to Joy. "You don't have to do this. I already told my office that you need a little time off."

"I need a whole lot of time, Dad. I'm not coming back. Matter-of-fact, I don't think I ever want to see you again." There, put that in your pipe and smoke it, Joy thought as she glared at her father.

"Don't do this, Joy. Okay, I know that you're upset with me right now. But don't forget who I am. My relationship with your mom might be over, but I'll always be your father."

"You are such a hypocrite, Dad. You want Dontae to understand the consequences for his actions and you want me to forgive and forget. But you don't seem to care at all that you're bailing out on a twenty-five year marriage. So tell us, Dad, what are the consequences for your careless actions?"

"What do you want me to say to that, Joy?"

"I want you to answer me. What are the consequences for your actions? Do you even feel the slightest bit guilty that your wife is in the hospital because of what you did to her?"

Nelson stood in front of his children with eyes that were void of answers. When the silence became

68

uncomfortable, he took his wallet and keys off of the kitchen counter and headed for the door.

"Dad, where are you going? I thought you wanted to make things right. You need to stay here with us. This is where you belong." Dontae was practically begging as he followed his father to the front door.

"Stop begging him, Dontae. He is not interested in us. He would rather be with a woman who only wants him for what he can give her, rather than stay with the woman who helped him get to where he is in the first place." The venom and contempt was laid bare in every word Joy spoke.

Nelson snatched open the door, but before he walked out, he turned back to his children and said, "Tell your mother that I have paid all of her bills and will continue to do so for the next three months. But if she wants to keep this house after the divorce, she'll have to find a way to pay for it."

When Nelson closed the door behind himself, Dontae turned to his sister, looking every bit the seventeen year old, rather than the grown man his height and muscles projected. "So that's it? He's just going to leave Mom to figure out a way to pay for this house?"

Joy wasn't about to let up on her father. She angrily pointed out, "And don't forget, this is the house that Daddy wanted in order to impress his peers. I guess he's decided that he doesn't care about impressing them, us or anybody else anymore. But you mark my words, Nelson Marshall will get his."

"How?" Dontae asked.

"Daddy isn't invincible, Dontae. And his job isn't secure at all. Judge Marshall has to be re-elected if he wants to remain a judge. Suppose it gets leaked to the papers that the so-called "family values" judge divorced his wife for his twenty-three-year-old mistress?"

Dontae rubbed his hands together. "Who can we call?"

Joy lifted her hands. "Hold up. Let's not be too hasty. Mom would never forgive us if we ruined her husband's career. But the minute he's not her husband," Joy shrugged, "all bets are off."

Seven

When Carmella woke the next morning, she didn't feel as if she was in a fog and couldn't think or make sense of anything. However, she was still in a bad place, mainly because she didn't understand why God had allowed all of this to happen to her. For more than two decades now she had loved and served God. Carmella had served in the choir, on the usher and greeter team and the marriage ministry.

Carmella thought that as long as she was handling God's business, He would, in turn, handle hers. But then her brother had a heart attack and died at the young age of forty six. She'd tried to deal with that tragedy by telling herself it wasn't God's fault that her beloved brother ate double and triple cheese burgers with bags of fries three to four days a week and was a hundred and fifty pounds overweight.

However, the problem Carmella now faced was that she was having a hard time not blaming God for the end of her marriage. It was His job to look after her, wasn't it?

Malachi 3:10 told her that if she gave her tithes to her church that God would pour out a blessing that she wouldn't have room to receive. But with the way things were going, it looked as if she had some extra room for some of them delayed blessings.

Her favorite bible verse came from Psalm 37:25: I have been young, and now am old; Yet I have not seen the righteous forsaken, Nor his descendants begging bread.

That verse always made her feel as if God had her back and that nothing could ever harm her or her children. But now that she knew God wasn't always on His j-o-b, what was she supposed to do now? Life had changed for her. But Carmella didn't know how to change with it. She didn't know how to live in a world where God no longer made sense to her.

For years she had projected the image of a super Christian who had it all together. Carmella had doled out so much God-centered advice to struggling Christians, that at times she wondered why she hadn't gone to school for counseling. But in her time of need, who did she have to guide or inspire her? Her parents were gone, her brother had recently joined them and even Nelson had left her. Carmella was searching for a reason to get out of the bed so she could leave the hospital. But the more she searched, the more she wanted to close her eyes and never open them again.

"Mom, you're awake!" Joy said as she and Dontae stepped into the room.

Carmella's eyes shifted towards the door, a brief smile crossed her lips as she watched her children walk into the room. "Hey, you two."

"Hey yourself," Dontae said as he walked over to his mother's bed. He bent down and kissed her forehead. "You had us worried yesterday. But you're looking more alert today."

Her teenaged son sounded so grown up, as if he had aged overnight. What was she doing with herself? Why was she lying in this bed and letting her children worry about her, when she should be the one worrying about them, like mothers normally do?

"Mom?" Joy's voice held concern after Carmella didn't respond to Dontae. "Are you okay?"

An involuntary tear rolled down her face as she said, "I'm trying to be."

"Dad fixed the faucet," Dontae told her in an upbeat tone.

Joy grabbed hold of her mother's hand and squeezed. "He paid the bills, too, Mom. So, you won't have to worry about that when you come home."

"Did he say if he was coming back home?" Carmella asked, hating herself for even needing to ask something like that, but she couldn't deny that she wanted her husband and her life back.

"He didn't stay at the house last night, but I'm sure he'll come back home, Mama. You just have to keep the faith, like you always tell us. Isn't that right, Joy?" Dontae looked to his big sister for support.

"Stop doing this to yourself, Dontae." She moved him away from the bed and told him to sit down. Joy then turned back to her mother and said, "Dad said that he's going to pay the bills for another three months, but after that you are on your own. I'm sorry to tell you this so flat out, but I don't want you to keep your hopes up for a man who may never come back to you."

"What else am I supposed to do, Joy? I've been married to your father for twenty-five years. My parents and my brother are gone… he's all I have."

Joy sat down next to her mother's bed and held onto her hand. "That's not true, Mama. You've got me and Dontae. And we will never leave you."

Tears sprang to Carmella's eyes. Her children brought her so much joy, and she never meant to insinuate that they weren't enough. As Joy and Dontae grew, she and Nelson made sure that they had all they needed and then some. From vacations to cars and education… you name it, her children had it, because Carmella required no less. She and her brother grew up in poverty. Carmella never wanted her children to experience the pain and embarrassment of being financially broke. But now she had allowed them to see her emotionally broken. As tears continued to fall down her face, Carmella wondered which was worse.

"Don't cry, Mama. I'm a dope. I shouldn't have said any of that to you today." Joy put her head in her hand and shook it.

"What Joy is trying to say is that we just want you to get better. Don't worry about what Daddy's doing. And you don't need to worry about the bills either because they've been paid," Dontae said.

There he was sounding all grown up again. Just two months ago she couldn't get him to stop playing his video games long enough to take out the trash, now he was admonishing her to keep the faith and encouraging her to worry less. Pretty soon he'd be leaving home, headed off to Harvard, his dad's alma mater. Carmella had imagined that she would convince Nelson to travel the world with her once Dontae was settled in college… she wiped away the tears, hating the fact that Nelson's betrayal hurt so much. "I'm sorry about losing it the way I did. Seeing your father with Jasmine just caused something to snap inside of me."

"It's been hard on you, Mom, we know that," Dontae encouraged.

But Carmella lifted a hand, stopping him from saying anything further. "I don't care how hard this is on me. I'm ashamed of myself for allowing you and your sister to see me like this. All I can do is apologize for what I've done and make a promise to both of you that once I get out of here, I'll never lose it like this again." Carmella had no idea how she would keep that promise, but she knew she had to say something to reassure her children.

The door opened and Rose walked in. "Well, don't you look alert this morning."

Carmella gave her friend a questioning glance. "Were you here yesterday?"

"You know it. The kids and I spent the day with you."

"Aunt Rose did more than spend the day with you. She sent us home and spent the evening in here praying for you," Joy told her mother.

"Is that true, Rose?"

Rose shrugged. "I didn't do anything that you wouldn't have done for me."

"I don't even remember anything about yesterday. Except that I felt as if I was in a fog and couldn't get out."

"That was because of all the meds they had you on. But Aunt Rose told me to make them stop medicating you," Joy told her mother. "We knew you'd feel better once you could think straight."

Carmella hoped that her daughter was right about that. After seeing Nelson with that man- stealing woman-child, and being laughed at for coming to get her own husband, Carmella had lost it. It was good to be able to lay there and talk with her children and her best friend. They spent the morning talking and then the nurse came in and told Carmella that she was being released.

"Thank the Lord," Rose shouted.

But Carmella didn't feel much like thanking the Lord, because she felt as if the Lord had let her down. Where had He been when Nelson was stepping out on her? Why hadn't the Lord allowed her to detect the clues that must have been there? And why had the Lord allowed Nelson to walk his narrow behind out of her life?

She didn't tell anyone how she was feeling. She just went home, climbed into her bed and lay there while Joy and Dontae fussed over her. The television was tuned in to the news and all of it seemed so depressing that Carmella couldn't take anymore. She began channel surfing, hoping to find something to put her in a better mood.

"Do you need anything?" Joy asked as she opened her bedroom door.

"I don't need anything, Joy. You just asked me that ten minutes ago. You and your brother need to chill. Go watch a movie or something."

"Okay, but if you need me, remember that I'm just downstairs." Joy looked anxious as she closed the door.

Carmella understood why her children were watching her like she was a kleptomaniac in a room full of fine china, but she needed time alone. She needed to think. Something she hadn't allowed herself to do much of since Nelson packed his bags and left. Carmella had been acting as if her life was over. But in truth, she still had a great deal to live for. Carmella just needed to find a way to let what she had left be enough. So far she hadn't figured out how to do that. But she was home and back in her right mind, so figuring out her new life would become priority number one, first thing in the morning. But tonight, she just wanted to veg out and watch television mindlessly for a few hours.

As she switched from channel to channel, she happened upon a Christian station, which reminded her that she hadn't been to church since this ordeal with Nelson began. Carmella didn't want to be preached at or feel convicted tonight, so she switched to the next station. It was another Christian station. But this one was showcasing a gospel concert. Carmella loved gospel music and would spend all day in the kitchen cooking and praising God while her praise music vibrated against the walls.

Recently though, when she'd gone into her beloved kitchen, it had only been to fix a quick meal, so she hadn't bothered turning on her gospel music. Nor had she bothered to praise the Lord while she went about her day. As she lay there watching and listening to the video of Deitrick Haddon singing Well Done, she realized that even after all that had happened to her, she still wanted to make it to heaven and wanted to hear God say well done.

As Deitrick asked, through song, if anyone wanted to see their loved ones again, tears dripped down Carmella's face as she thought of her parents and her brother, the loved ones she had lost and was positive that they had already heard the Lord say well done.

Carmella was amazed as she listened to the words of that beautiful song. But what disheartened her was the fact that the very same man who sang a song that could speak to the very heart and soul of the listener and cause them to want to do what's right in order to make it into heaven, had struggled in his marriage as well.

Nelson was awful for what he had done to her, but at least he wasn't a pastor or minister of the gospel. Just when she was starting to get angry, and plotting a beat down, rather than enjoying the song for the praise it sent up to God, the messenger left the screen and the song ended. Carmella knew that wanting to smash in the face of every man who ever had the audacity to cry out to God with the same mouth they asked for a divorce with, was not in any way, shape or form being Christ like. But she couldn't help how she was feeling. She also knew that God loved that singer just as much as he loved her and some times things happen in life. But that never destroys God's message of hope and love.

She was about to turn off the television and close her eyes to try to get her mind right, when the host of the gospel video fest started talking and it seemed to Carmella as if he was speaking directly to her.

He said, "Life is strange in that we can be praising God one moment and falling into sin the next. Or if we aren't the one committing sin, we are so busy judging the ones who fall into sin that God finds no pleasure in us either.

"In Galatians 6:1 it says, If a man is overtaken in any trespass, you who are spiritual restore such a one in a spirit of gentleness, considering yourself lest you also be tempted.

"What am I trying to say?" the announcer asked after quoting from the bible. "Whether you are the one caught up in sin, or you're the one watching and judging it, we all need to pray. And one more thing…"

He pointed at the screen in a manner that caused Carmella to believe that he was once again only speaking to her, "When you're in the midst of trauma and drama, don't forget to get your praise on."

With that said the video of Praise Him in Advance by Marvin Sapp began playing. He was one of her all time favorite gospel singers. He had experienced so much tragedy in his life, and yet he still praised God. Carmella had much respect for Marvin Sapp. So when his video came on, she lifted up on her elbow and leaned closer to the television. Then Marvin Sapp reminded her that praise was her weapon against her problems, because it confused the enemy. She had forgotten how to praise God as she began going through this situation with Nelson. Carmella could picture the devil laughing at her right now.

She didn't know how or why it happened, but Carmella was clear on something now: she was in a spiritual battle and the winner would get her soul. When she gave her life to God two decades ago, it had been because she wanted to make it to heaven. She may have forgotten that simple fact over the last month, but in truth, Nelson's leaving hadn't changed her mind. She still wanted to see Jesus, her parents, her brother and everyone else that was walking on streets of gold. Carmella just didn't know how to get back to that place of peace she had once known.

Come to Me. My arms are open wide, waiting for you.

It was like a sweet whisper in her ear, but Carmella knew that God had just spoken into her spirit. She was going to win the battle, because she was going to start praising God even before the storm was through raging, as Marvin Sapp's song advised.

The next video popped up and Mary Mary started singing about taking the shackles off their feet, Carmella flung the covers off, got out of bed and started dancing around her room. She was just getting started as that video ended and the announcer declared, "You got problems, you got pain? Well praise God anyhow and watch Him bring you through it all."

When Yolanda Adams's I Got the Victory came on, Carmella lifted her hands and praised the Lord like she hadn't in a long, long time. Each one of the performers that night had spoken to Carmella's heart in a special way, but Yolanda's words emboldened her. She had the victory alright, and she wasn't ever going to give it back.

"You can't have my mind and you sure can't have my soul." She was shouting at the devil that tried to destroy her life and with each step as she danced around her room, she was stomping on that serpent's head.

Her door swung open and Joy and Dontae ran in. "What's wrong?" Joy asked, breathlessly.

"What happened?" Dontae asked as he came in behind his sister.

Carmella's turned toward the door as her children rushed in. They had these worried looks on their faces, like they thought it was time for another seventy-two hour hold. "Relax, you two. I haven't cracked up again. I'm just praising God."

"What for?" Dontae asked as if that was the most ludicrous thing he'd ever heard.

"You've seen me praise God before."

"Yeah, but that was when you had something to praise Him for," Dontae said.

Her children didn't understand her. But Carmella couldn't blame them. She had been walking around like a woman with no faith for over a month. She'd allowed Nelson to strip her bare—but no more. "For the rest of my life, I will praise God whether things are right or wrong… whether I'm happy or sad."

"If you say so," Joy said with a raised eyebrow.

"What do you mean, if I say so? God is good, Joy Lynn and it's time we started appreciating Him for His goodness."

Both Joy and Dontae looked at her as if she'd just stepped off a space ship and asked them to take her to their leader.

She didn't have time for unbelief. Carmella was on an uphill climb, finding her way back to her Savior and she wasn't about to let her kids get her off track. She put her hands on her hips and told them, "Either praise God with me, or get out of my room so I can finish my praise dance."

"I'm not going to dance around this room looking crazy," Joy said as she turned and walked out of her mother's bedroom.

"Count me out, too," Dontae told her as he also left the room.

Carmella smiled, turned up her television and kept dancing. Because she'd realized something... not only did she still have her children, but as Joy promised, they would never leave her. Carmella also knew that God was still on her side and that he would never leave her.

Eight

Things weren't all good in her life, but Carmella was in a praise-Him-anyhow kind of mood and she prayed she would stay in that frame of mind for the rest of her life. Her children were having a hard time adjusting to their new normal and Carmella blamed herself for a lot of their struggles. If she had handled the separation better, then maybe Joy wouldn't have quit working for her dad or lost so much enthusiasm for law school. Dontae had started cutting classes and being disrespectful to his teachers. Carmella was still praying about the best way to handle that. With Dontae, if she pushed too hard, he would just shut down and she wouldn't be able to reach him at all.

She'd tried getting Nelson to spend more time with Dontae, but the man seemed completely ignorant to the fact that his own son was hurting. Well today was pay up day, as far as Carmella was concerned. Nelson wanted a divorce and after three months of waiting for him to come to his senses, she had come to hers.

Carmella hired a lawyer to represent her interests. Her neighbor, Cynthia had given her Deidre Green's information, stating that the woman was a pit bull. Carmella was on her way to meet with Deidre, Nelson and Clark Johnson, Nelson's attorney. Carmella was prepared to sign the divorce papers, but she wasn't about to go away empty handed. Not after working to put Nelson through law school and then helping him with every step of his career. Nelson might not know that he had her to thank for the advances he'd made, but thank God, since speaking with Deidre, she knew her worth—and he soon would, too.

As they sat around the table, Carmella nodded to the man who used to be both their attorney, "Clark."

"How've you been, Carmella?" he asked, his discomfort evident.

"I've been better. But you live on and you move on, right?" Carmella had learned how to motivate herself in the days since she got her praise back. Whatever doesn't kill you makes you stronger, and she was living proof of that.

Clark smiled. "You've got the right attitude about all of this."

Nelson was sitting quietly, looking down at his fingers as she and Clark exchanged pleasantries. But Deidre piped up and said, "We just hope your client brought the right attitude to this meeting. And by right attitude, I mean, he needs to be in the spirit of giving."

"I've already given. I've paid the bills the last three months. But it's time for Carmella to get a job. I can't keep supporting her when I'm not even in the house anymore."

Deidre quickly responded, "You're not home anymore because your girlfriend wanted you to move in with her. But that's not my client's problem."

Carmella had been terrified about life after Nelson. She'd been even more terrified about facing him in a head to head meeting to discuss the terms of their divorce. But after meeting with Deidre and going over her worth after years of cooking, cleaning, child rearing and generally making life happen for all the other members of her household, she became more confident in her abilities. God is good, because she never knew she was worth so much. Nelson leaving didn't scare her quite so much anymore. Carmella thought, Just as the bible says, if the unbelieving, cheating, stanking, no good husband doesn't want to stay, then let him go on, and let him live a miserable life with his gold digger... well, maybe the bible doesn't say all of that, but it does say to let the unbeliever go. But on the day that she was finalizing a divorce she never wanted in the first place, Carmella felt entitled to a little adlibbing.

Nelson glared at Deidre and then turned to Carmella. "Why'd you have to hire an attorney? Why didn't you just sign the papers and get on with your life?"

Again Deidre placed a hand on Carmella's shoulder. "Because my client is no fool, Mr. Marshall. The agreement you sent to Mrs. Marshall basically entitled her to six months of living expenses and no more. But you seem to forget that Mrs. Marshall put you through law school and cooked, cleaned, bore your children and washed your dirty clothes for twenty-five years. So, I'd say that's worth much more than six month's of living expenses, wouldn't you?"

"Mr. Marshall isn't a wealthy man. But he is more than willing to bump that up to a year's worth of living expenses. That ought to be enough to assist Carmella with this transition. Wouldn't you agree?" Clark asked.

Deidre opened the folder in front of her. She took her time looking over the information, then once the suspense had mounted, she said, "Based on the research we've done on your client's financials," she paused, looking like a woman who enjoyed her job, "with your position as a judge and your consulting business, you've been consistently earning about three hundred thousand a year. We're going to be asking for half of that for a period of no less than five years."

"What!" Nelson exploded. He turned to Clark and said, "Do something."

"Fifty percent does seem a bit over the top, don't you think, Mrs. Green?"

"Not at all, Mr. Johnson," Deidre answered without giving it a second thought. "Carmella isn't the one shacking up with a teenager, she's just the woman left behind… the one who put her life on hold in order to make all of your client's dreams come true. He wants to be set free, fine. But he has to pay."

"But I can't afford it," Nelson glanced in Carmella's direction, his eyes imploring her to understand his plight.

She looked at the man who'd sent her flying over the cuckoo's nest, the same man who had broken her children's hearts, all because he was a selfish and ungrateful human being and she felt no pity for him. "Tell your girlfriend to get an after school job, or learn to live with less."

"Why should I live with less? You're the one who hasn't worked for twenty years."

No he didn't. She didn't even recognize Nelson anymore. The man she had been married to used to thank her for the way she contributed to their family. The monster seated across from her was all dressed up like Nelson Marshall, but he had to be an impostor. "I no longer feel as if I know you, and since I prefer not to talk to strangers, I'm going to ask that you address my attorney for the rest of this meeting."

"So, now I can't even talk to you? Some wife you turned out to be."

Carmella didn't respond to him. She turned back to Deidre and asked, "Can you please continue?"

"Certainly." Deidre glanced at her paperwork. Checked off a few items and then said, "We want to have the college fund for Dontae Marshall transferred into either Carmella's or Dontae's name immediately."

"Oh, so now I can't be trusted to manage my son's college fund?"

"You're a busy man, Mr. Marshall. We wouldn't want that college fund to fall into the hands of your mistress because you failed to keep an eye on it," Deidre wasn't about to let up on reminding Nelson that he was the one committing adultery in their marriage. As far as she was concerned he could sit back, shut up and start writing checks, because he was going to pay for the way he discarded his wife.

Nelson and Clark leaned close to each other and said a few words, then Clark said, "Since Dontae is seventeen and will be going off to Harvard next year anyway, Mr. Marshall has no problem with turning the college fund over to his son."

Whether Dontae would be going to Harvard or not was still an open question, but she wasn't going to tell Nelson that Dontae was on the fence about which school to attend the following year. That was the reason she wanted the money out of Nelson's care. She felt that he was in no position to dictate to her son what he should and shouldn't do. And Carmella knew that Nelson would try to use the money to threaten Dontae. If it was up to Nelson, Dontae wouldn't get a dime if he decided not to attend Harvard. She'd sleep better knowing that Dontae had the freedom to follow his own path.

"One more thing," Deidre said as she held up her hand.

"There's more? What do I owe you now...my kidney? I mean we are splitting everything of mine 50/50 right?" Nelson was beginning to sweat. He loosened his necktie as he shook his head in disgust.

Carmella almost laughed in his face. With what he owed her, she could buy a kidney if she ever needed one. She was so thankful that Cynthia introduced her to Deidre Green. The woman knew her stuff and had opened Carmella's eyes.

"No, Mr. Marshall, we're going to let you keep your kidney. But we will take half of the two million that is currently invested in your retirement account. We will also be asking for half of your pension when you retire," Deidre told him with a sweet smile on her face.

"That is out of the question," Nelson barked. He looked at Carmella and asked, "How am I supposed to live? You're just being vindictive... I never expected this from you."

Clearly, Nelson hadn't expected Carmella to do anything but sign the divorce papers and let him go about his merry way. But her mom hadn't raised no fool. She knew how much was in every account they had, and after twenty-five years of service, if she was being set out to pasture, she was going in style. "I'm really not interested in hearing you whine. You want out, and I'm tired of begging you to stay. But you best believe that I am well aware of my worth. And I expect to get everything that's coming to me."

"Greed is a sin, Carmella. You know that, don't you?" Nelson glared at her.

"Starving to death should be a sin. Thank God I won't have to do that."

"Why don't you just get a job?" Nelson asked angrily.

"I had one, but it was stolen away from me," she shot back. Carmella was getting tired of this back and forth with Nelson. She felt her temperature rising and knew that anything else she had to say to him would not be Christ like, so she did her best to ignore him for the duration of the meeting.

Deidre passed the divorce paperwork to Nelson's lawyer. "I would advise your client to sign these papers. It's the best deal he's going to get."

"What about child support?" Nelson asked grumpily. "After I've given you all this money, are you going to then turn around and take me to court for child support?"

"Read through the documents. The child support is included in the fifty percent of wages we are asking for. Spousal support is slotted at thirty percent, and child support at twenty percent. Both will last five years, which is enough time to get your son through college."

"We will review it and get back with you," Clark said as he stood, tapping Nelson on the shoulder. Nelson stood and began walking out of the office with his lawyer.

Before they could walk out the door, Deidre added, "If I don't hear from you in a week's time, we will prepare for court. And at that time, we will ask the judge for fifty percent spousal support and twenty percent child support."

The door slammed behind them. Carmella hadn't realized that she'd been holding her breath, but as she released it, the tension in her neck and stomach began to ease. "Thank you," she said to Deidre. "I wouldn't have been able to get through this meeting without you."

"It was my pleasure."

"It looked that way. But I don't understand how you can enjoy meetings like this. Have you always handled divorces at your law firm?"

Deidre shook her head. "I didn't attend law school to become a divorce attorney. But fifteen years ago my father left my mother penniless, so he could marry his twenty-year-old receptionist. Mom killed herself right after my father announced his engagement." Deidre shrugged. "Ever since then I've been helping women get what they deserve out of these men who didn't deserve them in the first place."

Nine

In her kitchen with her praise music going and chocolate muffins in the oven, Carmella told Rose about her awful meeting with Nelson. She gave her a blow-by-blow account of how her husband had behaved.

"I'm proud of how you held up and fought back. Nelson is getting what he deserves. Only a slime ball would leave his wife the week after she had to bury her brother," Rose told her friend.

Carmella took her muffins out of the oven and began spreading her homemade icing on them. "It wasn't easy, girl. I was terrified to face him at first, but the more he opened his mouth, the more I enjoyed everything that was happening to him."

"Good."

Carmella brought a few of the muffins over to the counter island and sat down with her friend. "But you know, it did hurt when he questioned my Christianity. After what Nelson did to me, I had to struggle so hard to

94

regain my faith and my praise, and then he had the nerve to say that I'm too greedy to be a Christian."

"I know you're not letting that adulterer make you feel bad about anything." Rose took one of the chocolate muffins off the plate and bit into it. The gooey goodness of it melted in her mouth and caused a lingering, "mmmm" to ooze out of her mouth.

"I know, I know… You're right. It's just that after the battle I just fought trying to restore my faith, I don't want to hear anyone deny my right to call myself a blood-bought Christian."

"I hear you." Rose swallowed the rest of her muffin and then pointed at the plate. "Can I have another?"

"I thought you were watching your waistline?"

"Let my husband watch it. I'd rather eat another one of these delicious muffins." With that said, Rose grabbed another muffin and swallowed it in ten seconds flat. Her head went back and forth as she licked her fingers and she sang, "Mmm, mm, m."

Laughing, Carmella said, "I'm glad you enjoyed it. Maybe I should set up a table outside and sell the rest of these muffins to my neighbors as they drive by."

"Now why would you want to do a thing like that, when we could just sit here and finish them off ourselves?" Rose jokingly responded.

"To earn money, of course."

"You don't need to earn money, remember? Nelson is going to be paying your bills."

"That's only going to last for the next five years. I'm forty-seven years old, so I don't want to be facing the job market in my fifties. I need to figure something out now."

"Didn't you major in liberal arts in college?" Rose asked.

Carmella nodded. "I was supposed to go to graduate school so I'd be able to teach or something. But Nelson needed me to work so he could finish law school, so I never even got my teaching certificate. Now I'm at a loss as to what kind of career I can realistically expect to have."

"Well we both know that you love to cook. So, maybe you should be selling your muffins. Oh and don't forget about your cakes—and the pudding you make is to die for, too." Rose snapped her fingers, swung around in her seat and then said, "Matter-of-fact, I have the perfect venue for your first event."

"I'm all ears." Carmella leaned forward, anxious to hear what Rose had to say.

"I already have a caterer for the party Steven is throwing for clients in a few weeks, but we still need the sweet stuff. So, I am officially hiring you as my pastry chef."

Carmella was excited, but apprehensive. "Can you do that? I mean, would Steven be okay with you hiring me? I'm not a professional or anything." Rose's husband was an investment banker. His clientele would be top notch.

"Are you kidding? I wouldn't be able to find pastries better than yours. And if you're worried about looking professional, just give your business a name and order some business cards."

"Thank you, Rose." Carmella reached her arms toward her. "You are the best friend anyone could ever have. I don't know what I would have done without you."

"Are you kidding, Carmella? You are doing this all on your own. I've been watching you, girl, and you're reinventing yourself." Rose leaned over and hugged her friend. "I'm so proud of you."

When they finished hugging, Carmella said, "I just hope you're still proud after I deliver the pastries to your event."

Before Rose could respond, the telephone rang. Carmella hopped up and grabbed it. The caller ID told her that the call was coming from Dontae's high school. As she answered, she prayed that Dontae hadn't hurt himself in football practice like he'd done two years ago.

After she said hello, a deep rich, voice on the other end said, "May I speak with Mrs. Marshall."

"This is she," Carmella said as her toes began to curl. Even after all these years, she still recognized that voice.

"Oh, hi Carmella, this is Ramsey. I need to speak with you for a moment."

Ramsey Thomas had been her high school sweetheart. Everyone had assumed that they would get married and live happily ever after. Even her yearbook had been filled with well wishes for her and Ramsey. But after high school they had attended separate colleges. Ramsey met Pam and she met Nelson.

Ramsey's wife had died five years ago. Carmella had gone to the funeral and taken several cakes over to his house for the children. Two years ago Ramsey had transferred to Dontae's high school as the principal.

"How've you been, Ramsey?"

"I'm doing well."

"And the kids?" Carmella asked. If she remembered correctly, Ramsey and Pam had five children.

"I dropped the last one off at college last month, so I'm experiencing that empty nest syndrome. But I'll get over it… the kids are all happy and healthy."

Carmella felt for Ramsey. He and Pam should be having the time of their lives, traveling and doing things that couples couldn't afford to do during the early stages of marriage. But instead, Ramsey had to experience the joy and heartache of the last child leaving the nest all by himself. Life just didn't seem fair sometimes.

"I'm actually calling about Dontae," Ramsey said.

Carmella turned to Rose, lifted the one minute sign and then asked, "Has something happened with Dontae?"

"That's what I wanted to ask you." Ramsey hesitated for a moment and then trudged on. "I don't mean to pry, but since I've been at this school, I've heard nothing but positive things about Dontae from his teacher. But something changed this year. He's moody, getting into scraps with his classmates and he hasn't been turning in his work. Interim reports will be going out next week, and I guarantee that you will not be happy with what you'll see."

"Thank you so much for giving me a call, Ramsey. I know Dontae skipped a few classes. I talked with him and he promised not to do it again. I didn't know that he was having any other problems."

"His teachers started complaining to me about two weeks ago. I tried to talk to Dontae last week. But since I'm now getting ready to suspend him, I don't think he's listening."

"Suspend him! Why? What happened?" This is just going from bad to worse, Carmella thought.

"He got into a shoving match with one of his teammates."

Carmella put her hand to her mouth. She wanted to scream, but she refused to fall apart. Dontae couldn't have a suspension on his record, not with him being so close to getting into the college of his choice. "Is there anything else that can be done, Ramsey? Dontae knows better than this… especially now with all of his college applications sent out."

"Maybe Dontae thinks he's above the rules here since he's a senior. It might do him well to suffer the consequences of a suspension," Ramsey said.

Carmella shook her head. "It's not that, Ramsey. Dontae has been going through a lot lately. We all have." She took a deep breath and blurted out the facts. "Nelson left me and we're in the middle of a divorce. Dontae is having trouble dealing with the whole sordid mess."

There was silence on the line and then Ramsey said, "I'm sorry to hear that, Carmella. I had prayed for a lifetime of happiness for you and your family."

"Same old Ramsey, huh? Always thinking of others, even when you don't have to. Like my mother used to say, 'You must have been raised right.'"

"Brenda Thomas wouldn't have had it any other way."

She smiled.

Rose whispered, "What'd he say?"

Carmella waved her friend away and turned her back, so Rose wouldn't be able to see any more of her facial expressions. She asked Ramsey, "Is there anything else that can be done? Like making him wash all the faculty members' cars or something?" She held her breath for the answer.

"Now that I understand a bit more clearly what he's been dealing with, I think I can assign him to detention instead of suspending him."

"Thank you. Thank you so much for that, Ramsey. And when he gets home, I'll be taking those car keys from him until he can get his act together."

"I think that's a good idea. And Carmella…"

"Yes?"

"I'm sorry about Nelson."

She thanked him again for his kindness and then hung up the phone. Turning back to Rose, Carmella said, "I've got to figure out how to help Dontae get over what Nelson did to us before he ruins his life trying to get back at his father."

"The last thing you want him doing is messing up when he's so close to finishing school. You've got to do something quick," Rose said.

A devious smile crept across Carmella's face.

"What?" Rose asked.

"I'd been putting off repairs around the house, because I didn't have the money. But if Dontae isn't studying and isn't motivated to go to college anymore, he might as well get some experience in becoming a jack of all trades, so that he can earn a living."

"Oh, that's good."

"It's going to be all bad for him. Just wait until he gets home."

Ten

"Mom, why is Dontae outside cleaning the gutters?" Joy asked as she came into the house.

"Is that boy still working on the gutters?" Carmella opened the kitchen window and hollered for Dontae to come into the house. He came running while taking off his gloves. Carmella asked, "Why haven't you finished the gutters yet?"

"I just finished. I was on my way in to get my keys," Dontae told his mother.

"Keys?" Carmella picked up the rake that she had leaning against the wall. "You're not getting ready to go anywhere. There's a lot more work to do around here." She handed him the rake and informed him, "I don't want to see a single leaf in the yard when you're done."

"I've got homework, Ma. I can't be doing all this yard work."

"You weren't thinking about your homework a minute ago. You came in here to get your keys so you could go hang out with your friends," Carmella corrected.

"I was going over to Marco's house so we could study for our science test."

"Boy stop lying, you know you haven't been studying or doing any homework. Now get back outside and rake those leaves." She wasn't dealing with his foolishness. But one thing was for sure, by the time this week was over, her son was going to beg for the opportunity to study—and he would mean it.

Dontae walked back out of the house, dragging the rake and mumbling under his breath.

"What is going on around here?" Joy asked.

Carmella watched Dontae walk out the door, she then turned to Joy and said, "My son is trying to sabotage his future and I'm not going to let him."

Joy put her Louis Vuitton on the counter and sat down. "What's he done?"

"Besides fighting and goofing off in school, nothing much." Carmella sat down next to her daughter. "I failed you and your brother by falling apart after your father left me. But I'm not falling apart anymore and I'm not letting Dontae get away with this."

"What's your plan?"

"I'm going to work him like a Hebrew slave. When he's done with all the manual labor I have lined up for him, studying and getting into college is going to seem like a trip to Disney World."

"Okay Pharaoh, so when are you going to let Dontae go?"

"I don't know." Carmella tapped her fingers on the counter. "I'm just praying for direction and a miracle."

"Wow, I wonder what you're going to pray for when I give you my news."

Since leaving her apartment and moving back home, Joy had been nothing but a comfort to her. "Please tell me you haven't done anything crazy?"

"I don't think so, but I'm not sure how you're going to feel about it." Joy sat in silence looking at her mother, gaining the courage to say what came next. Then she opened her mouth and let the words trickle out, "I dropped out of law school."

"Have you lost your mind?"

"No, I'm completely sane and finally thinking for myself," Joy said.

Carmella stood up and ran her hand down her face. She was so mad that she wanted to drive over to Nelson's love nest and swing at him again. He got to run off with a girl half his age, while she got to stay home and put their family back together. "Think about this, Joy, you only have one more semester and you'll be done. Leaving school now might just be the biggest mistake of your life."

"Going to law school was the biggest mistake of my life. I only did it because Daddy wanted it so bad. But I'm done trying to please that man."

"Well, what does Troy think about this?"

Joy lifted her left hand, to show her mother that she was no longer wearing her engagement ring. "I gave the ring back. I'm not ready to get married."

"You can't just drop out of law school and call off your engagement without giving yourself time to think and pray about it." Carmella wrapped her arms around her daughter and kissed her on the side of her forehead and softly said, "Oh Joy, I know you've had to deal with a lot in the last few months by coming to terms with the end of your parents' marriage, but don't let him win… don't let him steal your dreams."

Joy's eyes filled with tears. She closed her eyes and the tears spilled over onto her cheeks. "I just need time to figure out what I really want, Mom."

"I know you do, baby, we all do," Carmella sat back down across from Joy and allowed Joy to lean her head on her shoulder. The two women then cried together until they couldn't shed another tear.

"What's going on?" Dontae asked as he came into the house. "Why are you and Joy crying?"

Carmella looked up. Her son was staring at her with fear in his eyes. He and Joy were fragile right now. She needed to make the right moves so that they could heal properly. Carmella was going to show compassion to her children, but she wasn't going to coddle them. The world wouldn't, so neither would she. She wiped the tears from her face as she told Dontae, "We're okay, we just had a moment."

"Are you sure you're okay?"

"Perfect." Carmella nudged Joy. "Isn't that right?"

Wiping her face also, Joy nodded. "I just needed a good cry. But I'll be all right."

Carmella then put her hands on her hips as she asked Dontae, "What's going on with the yard?"

"I did everything you asked. I've cleaned the gutters and raked the leaves. So, can I please go hang out with my friends for a little while?"

"How are you planning to get to your hang out spot?" Carmella asked, preparing to drop the hammer.

"I'm going to drive over there," he told her as he walked to the key holder by the garage door and noticed that his keys weren't there. "Who moved my keys?"

"I moved them," Carmella declared. "You're not driving until you bring your grades back up."

"Mom, why are you tripping," he whined. "My grades are fine."

"That's not what your teachers say. So I suggest that you make it your business to figure out what assignments you're missing and get them turned in immediately."

Dontae huffed and puffed, then kicked the counter.

"You might as well unflare those nostrils, because I couldn't care less how angry you are right now. But what you need to worry about is how angry I was when I heard that you'd rather fight than do your school work."

"Mr. Thomas told you about my detention, didn't he?"

"Told me about it? I had to beg him for it. You were getting ready to get suspended." She almost asked him what he thought the colleges he'd applied to would think about a kid who liked to fight rather than study, but she knew that was the point. Dontae was trying to self-destruct.

"He told you that?"

Carmella nodded.

"So when I told you that I had to stay late for football practice, you knew I was lying?"

"Don't you know by now not to lie to Mom? It's spooky how she figures stuff out. But I've learned to just 'fess up," Joy told her brother.

With a smirk on her face, Carmella picked up a can of white exterior paint and the paint brush that she'd placed on the kitchen table earlier in the day. "Enough chit-chat, I need you to paint the trim on the shed out back."

"What!" Dontae exploded. "Haven't I slaved around here enough today?"

"Don't complain, Dontae. I'm just trying to provide you with a skill."

"Why do I need a skill? I'm not trying to get a job; I'm still in high school."

"Look at it this way, Dontae, if you don't do your school work, you might not receive an acceptance letter from any of the colleges you applied to, so you'll need to figure out how to earn a living without a degree." She shoved the paint can toward him. "So here you go."

Rolling his eyes, Dontae took the paint and stomped his feet as he went back outside.

Joy started laughing. "I bet he won't do this again."

"I don't know what you're laughing about. I've got something for you to do also."

"Me... why?"

Carmella put a yellow notepad and pen in front of Joy. "Let's see... you quit your job a few weeks ago, you just dropped out of law school and you even broke up with your fiancé." Carmella ticked each item off with her fingers as she spoke. "You might be grown and can do what you want, but you are not sitting around this house, doing nothing."

"Okay, so what do you want me to do?" Joy asked, resigning herself to whatever task her mother might assign.

"I want you to help me plan my new business," Carmella announced.

Joy's eyes lit up. "What new business?"

"I'm going to be a pastry chef. I've decided to call my company Hallelujah Cakes & Such."

"Huh? I don't get it. Why would you add the word 'hallelujah' to a pastry business?"

"Think about it, Joy, the word hallelujah is the highest form of praise. And I have decided, come what may, I will live the rest of my life praising God for all He has done for me. So what better way to remind myself to praise the Lord, than to name my business something that indicates praise?"

Joy nodded. "All right then, Hallelujah Cakes and Such it is. So tell me, do you have a location for this business?"

"Not yet. I plan to operate right out of my own wonderful kitchen until I have enough cash flow to lease a location."

They talked for hours about the business, coming up with ideas and making plans for her first event. Carmella even let Dontae come in the house and get to his homework. But she wasn't finished with him.

Late that night, when Carmella finally made it to her bedroom, she fell on her knees and began praying. Her heart was full of so much animosity towards Nelson. The man was so selfish that he hadn't even taken a moment to worry about how his actions would affect his family.

"Lord Jesus, I'm putting Joy and Dontae in Your hands. You see the heartache and the trials they are dealing with. See them through this storm, Lord… they didn't ask for any of what is going on in our lives. Both Joy and Dontae adored their father, and I believe they are having such a hard time with our divorce because they have had to take their father off the pedestal they had placed him on. Help them to see that Nelson is just a man… a man who happens to be their father, and who still needs their love.

"But most of all, Lord Jesus, I am asking that You give them peace to ride through this storm. Give them direction for their lives and help them to come to know and love You as much as I do."

When Carmella was done praying, she began singing, "You are great… You do miracles so great"… and she believed every word she uttered. For God had truly been great in her life. He'd given her peace of mind and was even mending her heart. She'd never expected that she and Nelson would get a divorce, but with God by her side, she was determined to get through it. And even if she had to drag Dontae and Joy kicking and screaming, they would get through this horrible time in their lives also. In Jesus Name, she made that declaration.

She climbed in bed, turned on the radio that was next to her bed and drifted as a praise song lullaby her to sleep.

Eleven

Over the weekend Carmella did everything but beat Dontae like Toby and say, "grits dummy" to her son. By Monday morning Dontae told her that his body was aching from all the physical labor he'd endured, but that he wanted to go to school anyway. Carmella knew that Dontae thought the torture would end if he went to school, but she wasn't done with him yet.

Since Dontae wasn't allowed to drive until he pulled his grades back up, Carmella drove him to school. "This is lame, Mom. I have a reputation to uphold. How do you think it looks for people to see my Mom dropping me off at school?"

Carmella parked the car, turned the engine off and said as innocently as possible, "I hope the fact that I'll be auditing a few of your classes and helping out in the office this week won't drop your cool points with your friends."

Dontae inhaled and then exhaled slowly, making signs with his hands as if he was trying to get in a Zen kind of mood. "Please tell me this is a joke."

"No joke," Carmella said as she got out of the car. She began walking towards the front doors of the high school, but noticed that Dontae wasn't walking with her. She turned and saw him still sitting in the car looking about as miserable as a teenager could before being prescribed anti-depressants. Good, Carmella thought. He'll think twice before goofing off at school again. Carmella strutted back to the car, knocked on the passenger side window and yelled, "Come on, boy. We don't want to be late to your first class." Okay, she didn't have to keep rubbing it in, but she was determined to drive her point home.

"This ain't right," Dontae said as he got out of the car and stalked off toward the school building.

She closed her passenger door since her son left it wide open as if by magic, the door would close itself. Her Lexus SRX could do a lot of things, but closing its own doors wasn't one of them. She let Dontae rush ahead, because she needed to sign in before going into any of the classrooms.

The school secretary was at her desk when Carmella walked in. "Good morning, Mrs. Bell, how are you doing today?"

"Oh, Mrs. Marshall, how nice to see you. How've you been?"

"Things are going well," was Carmella's statement of faith. "I was hoping that I could audit a few of Dontae's classes today."

"I don't think that would be a problem. Just sign in right here." She pointed to the sign-in sheet. "And I'll get an approval for your day pass."

"I might want to come back a few more days this week if that would be possible."

Mrs. Bell smirked, getting the message. "Turning the screws on him, huh?"

"I'm throwing everything I've got at him, while still praying for a miracle."

"Okay, let's see if we can rustle one up for you."

Carmella sat down in the administrative office, waiting to receive her pass so she could stalk her son all day long. She only prayed that he would forgive her for what she was about to do. Maybe years from now when he became a huge success at whatever he decided to do with his life, he'd call and thank her for this—or maybe not.

Instead of the school secretary bringing her the day pass, Carmella looked up and saw Ramsey headed her way. She stood and gave him a hug, "Hey Ramsey, I didn't mean to bother you."

"No bother at all. You can have the pass and audit all of Dontae's classes, but I was hoping that we could maybe go about this another way."

"Like what?" Carmella asked, trying her best to concentrate. Ramsey was regal and gorgeous all at the same time. He was captain of the basketball team when they were in high school and she was on the cheerleading squad. That was many years ago, but she wanted to grab her pom-poms and give this brother a "Rah! Rah! Sis-Boom-Bah!"

"I can call Dontae down here and let him know that you've been okayed to attend all of his classes anytime you want."

Carmella was catching on. She added, "And then we can give him the opportunity to beg me not to do him like this and let him promise to do his work, right?"

"Right."

"Let's do it," Carmella said. She hadn't really wanted to humiliate her son, but she couldn't think of any other way to get her point across. Ramsey escorted her to his office and she sat down and waited for Dontae.

Ramsey sat down behind his desk and stared at her in a way that made Carmella squirm. "What?" she asked when he kept on staring.

"Nothing, I was just thinking that you're still the prettiest girl this high school has ever seen."

Was she blushing? Carmella hadn't blushed in years. Probably because Nelson hadn't said anything to make her blush in years.

Ramsey leaned back in his seat and kept going. "Looking at you, I feel like we're back in high school."

"Now you might as well stop lying, Ramsey Thomas. It's been twenty-nine years since we were in high school and I know I don't still look the same."

"You're right," he said with a gleam in his eye. "You look better."

Before she could respond, there was a knock at his door. Ramsey jumped up and opened the door. Dontae walked in.

"Mom, what are you still doing here?"

"I told you that I was going to audit your classes this week."

Ramsey held up a piece of paper. "I've signed off on her request and Mrs. Bell is about to print off a list of all your classes and the room number for each."

"Come on, Mr. Ramsey, help me out here. You know this isn't right," Dontae would plead for help from God Himself, if that was what it would take to get his mom to stop the torture.

Ramsey turned to Carmella and said, "I think what Dontae is trying to say is that he's kind of a big deal around here and having his mother checking up on him will make him look bad."

"I seem to remember someone else who was kind of a big deal around this school. When his mother visited this school, it caused him to straighten up and get his work done."

Ramsey's mouth hung slack and then he asked, "You remember that?"

"I sure do. And Mrs. Thomas was right in what she did…straightened you up."

"Yeah, but I was humiliated, Melly."

"The way you ran around this school acting like the king of the hill, you needed to be brought down a notch or two," Carmella told Ramsey with a hint of laughter in her eyes.

"Excuse me," Dontae said, trying to draw some attention back to him. "Did he just call you Melly? Am I missing something?"

Blushing again, Carmella told Dontae, "Ramsey and I went to school together."

"Oh okay." Dontae glanced at Ramsey and then back at his mother. He then got back to the discussion at hand. "Can you just please go home?"

"I don't think I'm ready to go home yet."

"Look Dontae, your mom has a day pass, so she can go anywhere in this school she wants. But if you want her to leave rather than follow you around today, then I suggest you ask why she's here and what she wants from you."

Dontae turned back to his mother. "Why are you here?" he asked while rolling his eyes.

She ignored his insolence. "Because I want you to win."

Dontae sat down in the chair next to his mother. "I don't understand what you're talking about, Mom. I don't get this at all."

She put her hand on her son's shoulder and gently said, "I know you're having a hard time with the divorce," her voice turned sharper as she added, "but that doesn't concern you as much as your school work does. I don't want you to mess up your last year of high school and then end up hurting your chances of getting into college."

"I'm not going to sit here and cry the way you and Joy cried the other night," Dontae told his mom as his lip slightly quivered.

"I don't want you to cry. I've done enough of that for the whole family. What I want you to do is strive to enjoy your life and keep getting the good grades you've always gotten." She put her forehead against his. "Can you do that for me?"

"If I promise to do my work, will you please leave?" A tear dropped from Dontae's eyes as the two continued to lean on each other.

Carmella pretended not to see the tear. "I'll leave now. Just do your work, okay?"

"Okay." Dontae stood up and turned his back on them as he wiped his eyes. "I gotta get back to class. I'll see you at home, Mom."

"Don't you need me to pick you up after school?" Carmella quickly asked.

"I'll catch the bus home." With that Dontae escaped.

Carmella turned back to Ramsey and said, "Thank you for that. Dontae might not have ever forgiven me for embarrassing him the way I had planned."

"I don't know about that," Ramsey had a grin on his face as he admitted, "I forgave my mom after my third year in college."

As she laughed, Carmella reminded him, "Remember how she busted up in our English class and was supposed to be sitting quietly. That lasted about ten minutes, until the teacher upset her by not calling on you to read any of the passages that we were going over that day."

Ramsey mimicked his mother as he said, "My son ain't no dumb jock. He can read, too. Show him, Ramsey... stand up and read something."

They both burst out laughing, then Carmella shook her head. "I can't believe that I was getting ready to do that to Dontae. But desperate times, call for desperate measures."

"But I have to admit that my head was pretty big when we were in high school. I just knew I was going to the NBA. If my mother hadn't convinced me that my education was important because nobody could ever take that away from me, I don't know where I would be now."

"You did play overseas for a few years, though," Carmella reminded him.

"I enjoyed playing overseas, but I couldn't stay there forever. So, when I got homesick, I was thankful that

I had finished college and only needed a few certifications to become a teacher."

Carmella was silent, but the sadness that crossed her eyes was unmistakable.

"Did I say something wrong?" Ramsey asked.

"Oh no, not at all. It's just that I had intended to become a teacher also, but it just didn't work out that way." She felt as if she was starting to bring down the mood with her woulda-coulda-shouldas, so she stood up. "I'm sure you need to get back to work, so I'll get out of your way."

"Actually, I was just getting ready to invite you to breakfast. There's an IHOP one block over."

Twelve

Carmella felt as if she were walking on clouds. Breakfast with Ramsey had been just what she needed. He made her feel young again, and reminded her of what it felt like to be cherished. Because one thing was for certain, she and Ramsey had loved each other. She had allowed herself to move on when she and Ramsey chose different colleges, because she had believed that teenage love wouldn't last. But now she was questioning that decision.

She'd given Ramsey her cell phone number and had boldly told him that the divorce papers would be signed soon, so he should feel free to call her. Carmella had been feeling so good that she even gave Dontae back his car kcys when he arrived home that evening.

Then things started going wrong. Carmella received a call from her attorney. She smiled as she noted the name on her caller ID. Deidre was probably calling to tell her that Nelson had signed the papers and she was free. It amazed her that she could smile about something that, only a few months ago, had seemed like being left behind after the rapture. But maybe she was doing some healing herself.

"Hey Deidre, how are you doing today?"

"Not so good, Carmella. I have some news that I really don't like delivering."

"What's wrong? Is Nelson still balking at the amount of alimony he'll have to pay?"

"He's refused to sign the papers, Deidre. He doesn't want the divorce."

Carmella sat down as she tried to wrap her mind around what she was hearing. Did Nelson really think that he could just call off their divorce as if it had just been a bad joke? "What do you mean? Does he think he can just come back home after all that's happened?"

"I don't think he's interested in coming home," Deidre said.

Now she was really confused. "If he doesn't want to come back home, why won't he just sign the divorce papers and get on with it?"

"They won't say. But Clark did let me know that Nelson is prepared to give in to all your demands as long as you let him postpone the divorce until December."

"But that's not fair. Why should he get to put my life on hold without even giving us a reason?" Carmella was outraged, pacing back and forth, wishing she had something to throw. She had already given Ramsey her number... had already started dreaming of a life without

Nelson and now he had the nerve to put her life on hold again. No, she wasn't going to stand for it.

"I think I know how we can get him to sign the papers."

"How?"

"I can tell his attorney that if he doesn't have those papers signed and in my office by the end of the week, we will go public with our story."

She was ready to be rid of Nelson, but she didn't want to do anything to cause him any problems. "I don't think I could do that, Deidre. I may not want to be his wife anymore, but I don't want to do anything to hurt him either."

"You are truly a woman after God's heart, Carmella Marshall. But I don't want you to worry about this. I said that I would threaten to go to the press on him —we don't actually have to do it. I'll call Clark back and let you know if I make progress with them."

After that call from her attorney, Carmella felt depression trying to set in again, especially after she'd received a call from Ramsey. He'd called to tell her how much he had enjoyed having breakfast with her and had asked if she would like to have dinner with him. Carmella wanted to scream yes from the rooftop, but she was still a married woman. She didn't want to play games with Ramsey and make him believe that she was just a signature away from divorce when Nelson was throwing her for all kinds of loops. She also didn't feel like letting him in on her melodrama, so she simply said, "Can I think about it and give you a call back?"

"Sure. I don't want to rush you. I know you're dealing with a lot right now."

Ramsey was so understanding and pleasant to talk to. How could she have ever thought her life would have been better without this man? It hurt so bad to say goodbye to Ramsey, because she felt as if Nelson was holding all the cards and she was once again powerless against him.

***

The next morning before getting out of bed, Carmella turned her praise music on while reading a few chapters in the book Joshua. When she reached the twenty-fourth chapter and fifteenth verse, Carmella felt convicted by her attitude as she read, as for me and my house, we will serve the Lord. She realized that Joshua had made a definitive statement that didn't take into account what might happen tomorrow or the next day.

Come what may, Joshua and his household would serve the Lord. And if serving the Lord for her meant staying married to Nelson and saying goodbye to Ramsey, then that was what she would do. However, she didn't feel as powerless the next morning as she had the night before. Because that morning after reading from the book of Joshua, Carmella knew that God would carry her through that time of uncertainty. Hadn't He helped Joshua fight the battle of Jericho by causing the walls to come tumbling down?

So, maybe God was at that very moment working to tear down Nelson's hard-hearted walls. Maybe God wanted her to give her marriage a chance by allowing Nelson a few more months come to his senses. The ironic thing was that since Nelson was delaying the process, she was the one who wanted it to move faster. Her heart had been changed and she no longer lived, slept and ate Nelson Marshall.

What scared Carmella, though, was that maybe it wasn't God that had brought about that change in her attitude towards her husband. Maybe seeing Ramsey and having him flirt with her and take her out to breakfast had moved her heart away from her husband. That wasn't right. Too many people lose their marriages because of wandering eyes. Carmella had too much respect for the institution of marriage to allow that to happen to her.

With her mind made up, Carmella had two calls to make before she started her workday. The first call was to Ramsey. She hadn't been truthful with him last night and Carmella felt that she owed him that.

He picked up on the first ring, and Carmella quickly said, "I know you're at work, so I won't keep you."

"Don't worry about it. This is my planning time, so I can talk for a while."

She cleared her throat as she gathered the strength to do what she believed was right. "I wanted to thank you for calling to check on me last night and for taking me to breakfast yesterday. That was the most fun I've had in a long time."

"Just imagine how much fun we'll have when I take you to dinner," Ramsey said.

He sounded as if he was grinning, and Carmella sure hated to take the smile off his face. "That's why I'm calling, Ramsey. I won't be able to go to dinner with you."

"Would you rather do breakfast again?"

"No Ramsey, that's not it. Nelson hasn't signed the divorce papers and has decided that he can't do it until December."

"What's going on, Melly? Didn't you tell me that the divorce was his idea?"

"I did and it is. I don't understand Nelson anymore, so I won't be able to explain the way his mind works. But I can't see you until I am actually divorced. You do understand that, don't you?"

Ramsey puffed out a long suffering breath as he said, "I understand. I don't like it, but I understand."

They hung up and Carmella made her next phone call. When her attorney got on the line, Carmella said, "Tell Nelson that the only way I will agree to postpone the divorce is if he agrees to attend marriage counseling with me."

"If that's what you want, I'll pass your demand along to them."

Carmella could hear the disappointment in Deidre's voice. But to her credit, Deidre held her tongue and handled her business.

Carmella then got dressed and walked out of her bedroom and went to her kitchen, her new workstation. Joy was already in the kitchen, pulling spices out of the cabinet.

"What are you doing up so early this morning?" Carmella asked her late-to-bed, late-to-rise daughter.

"Mom, it's nine-thirty. I could ask what you're doing getting up so late, but I could tell that you were in a bad mood when you went to bed last night."

Her children were still worried about her. Nothing Carmella said would convince them that they could stop worrying; she would just have to show them one day at a time. "I was upset, but I prayed about it and I'm just going to let the Lord handle it."

Joy left her spot by the cabinets and sat down at the counter. "I was doing inventory on all your spices, so we'd know what to pick up at the store for these cakes you want to bake."

"Thanks for getting on that, Joy. I can't believe my first event is only a week away."

Joy grabbed her mom's hand and gave her a serious stare down as she asked, "Do you want to talk about what upset you last night?" When Carmella seemed to hesitate, Joy added, "You'll feel better if you just get it off your chest… no more letting stuff fester, okay?"

"Okay Joy, no more letting stuff fester." Carmella sat down next to her daughter, she breathed in deeply and then said, "I was upset last night because your father has all of a sudden decided that he doesn't want to sign the divorce papers until sometime in December. But after praying about it this morning, I called my attorney and told her that I would agree to it if he would agree to go to marriage counseling with me."

Joy shook her head. "Mom, don't take this wrong, but for a smart lady, you are very naïve."

"I'm not being naïve, Joy. I'm just trying to do what I think God would want."

Joy closed her eyes, leaned her head back and as she reopened her eyes, she said, "Has it slipped your mind that the election is next month?"

"What does that have to do with anything?"

"Think, Mom. Daddy has probably had some advance polling done and he now realizes that he would most likely lose the election if he divorced you right now. My guess is, he'll be ready to sign the papers the moment he is re-elected to his judgeship."

"I don't think that your father is as cold and calculating as you seem to believe. And neither you nor I know what the Lord has to say about this matter, so I choose to wait to find out."

"Suit yourself, Mom. I hope it turns out the way you want it to."

"Me too," Carmella said, without indicating which way she wanted things to turn out.

Thirteen

Feeling like a fool, she sat in her pastor's office waiting for Nelson who was an hour late. She glanced at her watch one more time and then said, "I'm really sorry about this, Pastor Mitchell. Nelson told my lawyer that he would come to this counseling session. He must have changed his mind and just didn't bother to let me know."

"These things happen sometimes, daughter."

She had been a member of this wonderful church for twenty years. Pastor Mitchell was twenty-five years older than she, and he always called her daughter whenever they spoke. Being that her father was long gone, it made Carmella feel all warm inside every time she heard him address her as daughter. She wanted to put her head on his shoulder and cry her eyes out as she told him about all the problems she'd been having with Nelson and the kids.

Instead of doing that, she put her purse on her shoulder and stood. "Sorry to have wasted your time, Pastor. I think I'll just head on home now."

Pastor Mitchell came around his desk and took Carmella in his arms, giving her a warm, caring hug and asked, "How are you holding up?"

His shoulder was there, so she leaned her head on it and let a few tears seep out. "It's been hard, Pastor. I was caught off guard by this divorce, because I thought Nelson and I would be together until one of us buried the other."

As they moved apart, Pastor Mitchell patted her on the back while shaking his head. "I hate divorce. But if you've done all you can do, then rest in God, daughter. Let's see what He says the end of this matter will be."

Carmella was upset when she left church, but by the time she drove home, she had almost convinced herself that God was working this thing out for her, so she didn't need to stress over anything. But then she went inside her home and had to face her children.

Joy was the first to pounce. "So how was the counseling session?" She looked at her watch and then commented, "With all of Daddy's issues, I would have expccted ya'll to be there all night."

"Shut up, Joy," Dontae said as he rose with hope in his eyes. "Just let Mom tell us what happened."

Carmella wondered if Nelson knew just how much Dontae needed him to do the right thing. If for no other reason, she would hold on as long as she could so that

Dontae could get his hero back. But now she would have to tell them the truth. She put her purse and keys down and then said, "Your father didn't show up."

"What do you mean? He agreed to the counseling session, right?" Dontae asked.

"He did agree," Carmella answered her son, while looking at Joy. And if she wasn't mistaken, Carmella saw disappointment on Joy's face. It was as if she had lost all faith in her Dad, but was still secretly hoping that he would restore her faith. She tried to sound bright and cheery as she said, "Look, I don't want you two worrying about this. I'm sure Pastor Mitchell will allow us to reschedule the meeting. I'll just call Nelson and get a time that works for him."

"Stop it! Stop it!" Joy screamed at Carmella.

"I don't know why you're so upset with me, Joy. I haven't done anything. I'm just trying to make this right for all of us."

"Don't worry about us, Mom. You need to make this right for yourself." Joy was still yelling as she added. "Daddy is playing you for a fool. He's just stringing you along until the election. Don't you get it? He's never coming back home."

Carmella was getting a headache. Why had Nelson thought it was okay to leave her to handle the fall out of the mess he created. She couldn't take much more. Lord Jesus, I am weak, so I need You to be strong for me, she silently called out to her God as she sunk down onto the sofa in the living room and began rubbing her temple.

"Mom, don't stress," Dontae admonished. "We know you've tried to work with Daddy. It's his loss, though."

If it was Nelson's loss, Carmella wondered why she felt so lost and alone. Help me, Jesus!

"That's it. I'm going to handle this myself," Joy said as she stormed out of the house.

***

The next few days sped by as Carmella and Joy worked on the final preparations for her first paid event at Rose's dinner party and Dontae busied himself with homework and football practice.

It was the day of her event. Carmella had her business cards and she was putting the final touches on her cakes, pies, pudding and two different kinds of brownies. Her radio was on and Carmella was praising the Lord as she decorated her cakes. Joy had her checklist out and was busily counting the items and checking things off of her list. The praise music stopped as the radio station went to breaking news.

The newscaster said, "With the election coming up, here are some things we thought you ought to know…"

Carmella was stuffing frosting into a Ziploc bag. She cut a hole in the bag and frosted her pastries as the radio announcer talked about one issue after the next that affected North Carolina residents. The announcer then said, "And we have it on good authority that Judge Nelson Marshall, the same man who is running for re-election as a judge who will fight for family, has evidently stopped fighting for his own. Because he has left his wife and is now living with his pregnant girlfriend."

The frosting bag in Carmella's hand dropped, as her hands went to her mouth. She had no idea that she would be this devastated to hear that Nelson had gotten another woman pregnant. "Oh my God," she said as she started backing away from the table. She wanted to run to her bedroom and lock the world out as she digested this news.

"Mom, wait," Joy said, as she grabbed hold of her mother."

"I just need a moment, Joy. I'll be back, okay?"

"No, I don't want you to go." Joy hugged her mother. "It's not true, anyway. Jasmine isn't pregnant, so don't get upset for nothing."

Carmella pulled away from her daughter and then glanced over at the radio. "But they just said—"

"I gave that information to the media. I never told them that she was pregnant, but I insinuated it."

Carmella sat down. She lowered her head as she inhaled and exhaled. As she calmed herself, she turned back to her daughter. "Why would you do something like this, Joy?"

"Instead of asking me why I would do what I did, why don't you ask him how he could have done all this to you?"

"You had no right to put our business out there for everyone to hear. How do you think this makes me feel? Now I have to go to this party tonight and face all of these people while trying to get business from them." At this point Carmella wanted to call Rose and cancel. If this event had been for anyone but Rose, she would have done just that. She took a deep breath, decided to put one foot in front of the other and move forward.

Carmella got back to putting the frosting on her items. She tried her best to ignore Joy as she floated around the kitchen. But alas, Joy would not be ignored.

"I'm sorry, Mom. Don't be mad at me."

Carmella shook her head, still steaming at what Joy had done.

"I did it for you, Mom."

Carmella gripped the edge of her prep table as she told Joy, "I never asked you to humiliate me. Nor did I ask you to lampoon your father's chances of getting re-elected."

"He doesn't deserve that job. He's a hypocrite."

Carmella blew out an exhausted breath. "Joy, one day you are going to have to find a way to forgive your father. I don't want you going through life bitter and unyielding."

"I'm not bitter and unyielding," she declared.

Carmella held up a hand. "I don't have time for this right now. Let's just finish getting everything together and get through this event." Before turning back to her pastries, Carmella pointed a stern finger in Joy's face, "But I'll tell you right now, Joy Lynn Marshall, I'm going to make sure that you are the one passing out the pastries tonight. I'm going to stay at my station and let you handle all of the people who want to tell you how sorry they are about your dad."

"It's the least I can do for you, Mom. And again, I'm sorry that I embarrassed you. I hadn't thought about the other side of this story when I was passing it on to the media."

***

Rose's party was fabulous. And even though Carmella worried about receiving pity comments from the guests at the party, no one bothered them. She passed out her business cards and received orders from five of the guests. As they were driving home, Carmella's phone rang.

It was Deidre. Carmella pushed the phone button on her steering wheel and said "Hello?"

Deidre's voice traveled through the car as she said, "I have good news. Nelson signed the divorce papers."

Joy rolled her eyes.

"Are you kidding?" Carmella said, "I thought he didn't want to sign until after the election?"

"Apparently, having everyone know that he's living with his girlfriend without the benefit of a divorce from his wife is a big problem for his career goals," Deidre said.

"Okay, well thanks for letting me know."

"You don't seem happy," Joy said with a worried expression on her face.

"I doubt if anyone is happy when their marriage comes to an end. And I had been married to your father for twenty-five years." A tear flowed down her face as they pulled into the driveway. "I'll be all right," she told Joy as they got out of the car.

Carmella went to her bedroom, took a shower, threw on a pair of pajamas and then climbed into bed. She turned on the radio next to her bed. Let the Church Say Amen by Marvin Winans was playing and Carmella thought the sound was fitting for that evening. God had indeed spoken, her marriage was over and all she could do was say, "Amen".

Joy ran into her room. "Mom, turn on the news."

She turned the television on. Joy hurriedly put it on the news channel and Carmella saw Nelson being interviewed by a reporter, and he had the nerve to say, "Look, what could I do? My wife hired a lawyer and made all types of demands for a divorce. We'd been married for twenty-five years, but since she seemed ready to divorce me, I had no choice but to move on... and just for the record, I do not have a pregnant girlfriend."

"Can you believe him? He's putting the divorce on you, as if it was your idea."

"He's trying to save face. But it doesn't bother me. Now let me make a quick call and then get some sleep, okay?"

"Are you sure you're all right?"

Carmella nodded.

Joy left the room.

Carmella picked up the phone and dialed the number she'd wanted to dial from the moment she heard that she was a free woman. Life had thrown her for a loop, but thank God she was confident that she would be landing on her feet.

Ramsey answered the phone and said, "I'm so glad you called. My fingers were itching to call you, but I wasn't sure if that was the right thing to do or not."

"Well, did you pray about it?" she asked, holding her breath, waiting for the answer.

"I've been praying about us for a few weeks now. I've already gotten my answer; I'm just waiting on you to get on board."

"Nelson signed the divorce papers, Ramsey." She was a bit breathless as she made this declaration. Carmella could hardly believe the excitement growing in her at the thought of beginning again… with Ramsey.

"So, how about dinner," Ramsey said.

She could hear the smile in his voice again. This time she wasn't about to do anything to remove that smile. "I'd love to go to dinner with you."

"Okay, let me make the reservation and I'll let you know where we'll be eating. Is tomorrow night okay with you?"

"Tomorrow is perfect."

Carmella put the telephone back on the receiver and turned up her radio. They were playing Take Me to the King by Tamela Mann. Carmella pulled the cover over her body, exhaled as she laid everything at the feet of her King and then went to sleep, excited to see what tomorrow would bring.

Epilogue

After only three dates, Ramsey asked Carmella to marry him. But she said no. Perplexed by the matter, Ramsey took Carmella's hands in his and said, "But we love each other. I can see it in your eyes, Carmella. You never stopped loving me."

"I do love you so very dearly, Ramsey. You are the man of my dreams, but I'm on a journey with God right now, and I don't want to stop until it's finished."

"You and I have so much in common, especially our love for God... Let me go on this journey with you."

She pulled her hands away from Ramsey's, and lightly touched his beautiful face. Carmella wanted to marry this man like she wanted to get up every morning and sing praises to the Lord. But she loved Ramsey too much to accept his offer at this moment in her life. "I can't ask you to fix what another man has broken. I need to spend this time with God to heal myself and my children; can you understand that?"

Reluctantly, he nodded, leaned his forehead against hers and asked, "So what do we do now?"

She was tired of crying, but tears formed in her eyes anyway. "I have no right to ask you to stick around, or to wait on me to resolve my issues, but I sure wish you would."

He kissed her, and then held her in his arms, not wanting to let her go. "I'm not going anywhere," he told her.

Carmella was comforted by Ramsey's words, but there was another man on her mind who she very much wanted to go somewhere, but it appeared as if his life had stalled on him. Dontae had received his acceptance letter from Princeton. Then a rejection letter came from Yale, but most importantly he then received an acceptance from Harvard, his father's alma mater. But neither the acceptance nor the rejection moved him. Dontae seemed stuck. Carmella kept praying, but she was at her wits' end as to how to get him to move forward with his life.

But one day while she and Joy were working on a pastry order at her prep table, Dontae came running into the kitchen, full of smiles and all bubbly as if he'd just been put in the running for the Heisman trophy. "Mom, you won't believe," he told Carmella as he grabbed her arms and swung her around.

Carmella grabbed a towel and wiped her hands off. "Boy, what in the world has you in such a state?"

He had to catch his breath, but when he did, he said, "A scout for the University of Alabama came to my football practice today. They want me to play, Mom. They're going to give me a scholarship!"

Joy started jumping around the kitchen now. "Oh my God, Dontae, I'm so happy for you."

But Carmella was puzzled. "We never discussed Alabama. I thought you were going to pick between Harvard and Princeton. Both those schools want you. Even if you don't want to go to your daddy's old school, why not go to Princeton? Do you know how many kids spend their lives wishing and praying for this opportunity?"

A little bit of light went out of Dontae's eyes as he turned back to his mother. He shook his head. "I don't want either of those opportunities, Mom—at least not for my undergrad. I want to play for the Crimson Tide, and they want me. This is the best news I've received all year long. Can't you just be happy for me?"

What was she doing? Hadn't she asked God for a miracle for her son? How had she been so boneheaded as to think that the miracle had been when Dontae received acceptance letters to two colleges that he didn't want to go to in the first place? The miracle was standing right before her, his excitement about being able to play football for his favorite college team. Carmella would not be a foolish woman and continue arguing her point. She was just going to say Amen and get out of the way. "Well, I guess I'll have to sell a ton of cakes and pies so I can fly to all of these Alabama games."

At hearing those words, Dontae and Joy began jumping around the kitchen, again, giving each other high fives and doing dances that Carmella didn't recognize. She stepped back and watched her children. Nelson had left them, but God would never leave. This was why happy moments like the one they were having now were still possible.

"One down and one more to go," Carmella silently said to God as she lovingly glanced at her beautiful, big hearted, but bitter daughter.

Later that night as Carmella and Joy sat in front of the television watching the Cooking Channel, Carmella noticed that Joy wasn't as interested as she in what the chefs were doing and she made a decision. Carmella turned to her daughter and said, "I want to thank you for helping me get my business started."

"It's been fun; don't worry about it."

"You're fired," was all Carmella said next.

Joy had been slouching on the sofa. She shot up. "I'm what? How can you fire your own daughter? And on what grounds? I have been a model employee… and if I haven't been, you never told me anything was wrong."

"Listen at you… arguing your case. Don't you see, Joy? You weren't meant to follow my dreams. You have to follow your own, and I know that you love the law. You'd be an excellent lawyer."

Joy shook her head. "That was Daddy's dream for me."

"No, baby. Your father might be good at a lot of things, but he can't put something in your heart that's not already there."

Joy's fists curled as she punched the sofa, bitterness ruling her life. "I can't do it. Daddy gets everything he wants. He won the election, even after I told the media how horrible he has been to you. If I finish law school, he's won, and I don't want that."

Carmella wagged a finger in her daughter's face. "Now you listen to me, Joy Lynn, you let the good Lord handle your daddy, because you can't live with all this bitterness pumping through your veins."

Joy shrugged, not caring how childish she appeared.

"And contrary to what you believe, your not finishing law school does not make you the winner... you're the one losing out, because it's the thing you want more than anything."

They sat in silence for a while, Joy rolled her eyes and harrumphed a few times, but in the midst of it she must have been mulling things over, because when she finally spoke to Carmella again she said, "If I did go back to law school, maybe I could practice family law and help women like you when men like my father try to do them wrong, the same way Deidre helped you."

Carmella nodded. "You could do that, if that is truly where your heart is." She stood up and handed her daughter the remote. "I'm going to bed."

"You mean, you're going to call Ramsey," Joy said as if her mother was a teenager and she was the parent.

"I'm going to mind my own business and I suggest you do the same," Carmella told her as she headed upstairs to do exactly what Joy had said. She missed hearing Ramsey's voice and had to know that he was still there for her. As she picked up the phone, Carmella realized that she had had three love affairs in her lifetime.

She'd loved Nelson for over twenty years, but now that love affair had come to an end. Ramsey had been her first love, and he was back in her life to stay this time, she hoped. But the third love affair had turned out to be the most important of all; it would be an enduring one, forever after. She didn't have to wonder or guess about this love, because it was the love she shared with her Lord and Savior, Jesus Christ... all else would be secondary from here on out in the Marshall household.

The end

Join me on Twitter: https://www.twitter.com/
vanessamiller01
Vie my info on Amazon: https://www.amazon.com/
author/vanessamiller

Books in the Praise Him Anyhow series
Tears Fall at Night (Book 1 - Praise Him Anyhow
Series)
Joy Comes in the Morning (Book 2 - Praise Him
Anyhow Series)
A Forever Kind of Love (Book 3 - Praise Him
Anyhow Series)

Ramsey's Praise (Book 4 - Praise Him Anyhow
Series)

Escape to Love (Book 5 - Praise Him Anyhow Series)

Praise for Christmas (Book 6 - Praise Him Anyhow Series)

His Love Walk (Book 7 - Praise Him Anyhow Series)

Joy Comes in the Morning

Excerpt of Book 2 In

THE PRAISE HIM ANYHOW SERIES

By

Vanessa Miller

ONe

Psalm 137: 1-4

By the rivers of Babylon, there we sat down, yea, we wept, when we remembered Zion. We hanged our harps upon the willows in the midst thereof.

For there they that carried us away captive required of us a song; and they that wasted us required of us mirth, saying, "Sing us one of the songs of Zion."

How shall we sing the Lord's song in a strange land?

Joy Marshall strutted into the Municipal Courthouse at 8:55 am, just minutes before the judge would be seated. She was wearing the Michelle Obama sleeveless dress look. And since she was a P90X workout girl—with the t-shirt to prove it—Joy had the arms to carry off such a look. Her hair was pulled up on top of her head, giving her face an exotic look that caused the law breakers and the law makers in the courthouse to stop and stare. But Joy didn't even notice. She had one thing on her mind that morning… revenge. As far as Joy was concerned, revenge was best when served cold and she was about to serve up a heaping pile of it.

She hadn't spoken to her father in five years. He'd shown up at her law school graduation four years before, and Joy had turned her back to him when he tried to congratulate her. Her father had sent roses to her office when she had accepted an Assistant District Attorney position a year and a half ago, but Joy had sent the roses back. She'd also sent him a very unflattering picture of herself hugging a toilet and puking up her guts. She'd told her father that the picture represented the girl he had created… but he could never lay claim on the woman she would become.

Ramsey, her stepfather had taken that picture of Joy after one of her famous nights of drinking. The next morning he took her to breakfast at the same IHOP he'd taken her mother on their first, unofficial date. While Joy struggled to hold her head up, Ramsey slid the picture over to her. After taking a quick look at the picture, Joy's head started pounding. She ran her hands down her face, as a look of embarrassment crept up. "Where'd you get this?"

"I took it when you came home last night. I wanted you to see what a fine and upstanding woman you turned out to be."

She heard the sarcasm in his voice and didn't like it one bit. "Marrying my mother doesn't give you the right to get in my business. I'm a grown woman and prefer to be treated as one."

The waitress placed scrambled eggs and bacon in front of Ramsey and pancakes in front of Joy. When the waitress left their table, Ramsey said, "I'm not in the habit of treating people who live in my house like grown folk when they don't pay bills, and do nothing with their lives."

"I finished law school. Isn't that what my mother wanted? Okay, I did it, so stop harassing me."

Ramsey leaned back in his seat. He studied her for a moment and then let her have it, no holds barred. "Look Joy, I know that this adjustment has been hard on you... probably harder on you than anyone else, but you can't self-destruct over it."

What did he know about the pain she was dealing with? As far as Joy was concerned, her father hadn't just betrayed her mother when he cheated with Jasmine. He'd betrayed her as well, because she had looked up to her father and believed he could do no wrong. And then one day she discovered that he wasn't just doing wrong, but he was doing it with Joy's best friend. So in one crazy and heart-wrenching day, she'd lost not just her father and best friend... she'd lost her trust in mankind. And no matter how hard she tried, Joy just couldn't figure out how to get it back.

"Joy, I know that you're angry with your father, and you're trying to punish him for what he did to you. But you're going about this the wrong way."

Her stomach was not in the mood for food, so she pushed her plate away. But she was finally ready to listen to Ramsey. "What do you mean?"

"Success is the best revenge, Joy. Drinking yourself into an early grave is not going to hurt Nelson Marshall. You know what will stick in his gut, though? Show your father that you succeeded even though he chose to walk away."

Ramsey's words had so encouraged her, that Joy stopped drinking and put an honest effort towards finding a job. Now she was an Assistant District Attorney and today was the day that she would finally exact her revenge on her father.

The so-called Honorable Judge Nelson Marshall had been assigned to preside over her most recent case. When he saw her name, he should have recused himself on the spot, but since he chose not to do the right thing, as usual, Joy was about to do it for him.

"Good morning, Ms. Marshall. You're looking good today," a big bellied security guard, who obviously needed Ramsey to give him a good talking to so he could lay off the beers, said to her as she walked over to the security area.

"Thanks, Malcolm, how are you doing this morning?" Joy handed her Michael Kors handbag and briefcase to the security guard and prepared to go through the metal detectors.

"I'm doing good. Getting married next week," Malcolm told her as she walked through the metal detector.

Joy almost offered her condolences. But she reminded herself that not everyone viewed marriage as an apocalyptic occurrence. But they knew just as well as she did that over half of all marriages end in divorce. That includes the ones that claim to be Christian marriages, like the one her mother and father had, until the day he decided to leave her for his girlfriend. After her father had done his dirt and divorced her mother, Joy hadn't been able to look at marriage the same way. She'd even called off her own engagement to Troy Daniels and she'd been living happily single and not interested in mingling at all ever since. She didn't have time to go over all of her woes with Malcolm, so she simply said, "Congratulations. I wish you the best." Joy took her belongings and walked away from him as fast as she could.

Joy got on the elevator heading to the third floor. She walked into courtroom A, where Lance Bryant and his repeat offender were already seated and waiting on Judge Do-Wrong to make his royal appearance.

She caught Lance staring at her as she made her way to the prosecuting table. He was a fine brother with wavy hair and a beautiful smile, but she wasn't interested. Joy put her briefcase down as Lance leaned her way and said, "Long time no see... how've you been?"

Joy gave him a close lipped smile and then turned back to her paperwork. She had tried two other cases against Lance in the short time that she had been an Assistant DA. Lance seemed like a good guy, but he sure picked some loser clients. He handled everything from assault to robbery, and always seemed to believe that his clients were as innocent as new born babes.

"Oh, so it's like that, huh? You not speaking today? Guess you're still upset about that whuppin' you took the last time."

She'd won the first case, but Lance had, indeed, won the second case. Joy was actually thankful that Lance won that case, because as it turned out, his client had been falsely accused. But he wasn't about to win this case, not even close, nor was she about to deal with her father the entire week that it would take to wrap this case up.

"All rise," the bailiff said as Judge Nelson took his seat behind the bench.

Joy's fists instantly clenched as she watch her father sit in a chair he didn't deserve to be in. She had tried her best to get him out of that seat during the last two elections, but the people of North Carolina just kept voting the adulterer back in. A few years back, Joy had delighted in telling her father that she had been the one to provide the media with information about his girlfriend and his divorce. He'd tried to apologize to her for what he had done to their family, but she wasn't interested in hearing it.

Judge Nelson shuffled a few papers around as he avoided looking in Joy's direction. He then said, "All we are doing today is setting bail, so let's get to it."

Joy said, "I am not prepared to have a bail hearing yet."

Nelson took his glasses off and glanced in his daughter's direction. "What's the problem, Counselor?"

Joy smirked. Using the court in this manner could seriously damage her career, but she didn't care. Every chance she got, she was going to let her father know what an awful human being he was, and if anyone had a problem with it, she would simply start her own law firm. "You are the problem, Your Honor." As she said the words *Your Honor*, her eyes rolled and it was obvious to all present that she thought he was anything *but* honorable.

Nelson Marshall seemed to shrink in his seat for a moment. He closed his eyes and rubbed his temples. "This is not the time or place for this, Joy. You have a job to do and so do I. Let's just get on with it, all right?"

"No," Joy said flippantly. "You should have recused yourself from this case the moment you saw that I was the attorney of record, but since you didn't, I am now publicly asking that you recuse yourself."

"Am I missing something?" Lance asked as he looked from Judge Marshall to Joy. His client nudged him, and then whispered something in his ear.

"I see no reason why I should recuse myself. I am more than able to be an impartial judge in the matter that is before the court."

"It is well known that I informed the media about your marital misconduct, so if you do not recuse yourself, I will request a judicial review."

Lance lifted his hand in order to get the judge's attention. When Judge Marshall turned to him, Lance said, "If there is some sort of problem between you and the assistant DA, then I respectfully request that Attorney Joy Marshall recuse herself so that we can move forward with the case. My client is entitled to his day in court and he does not want to delay the process waiting for another judge to be assigned to the case."

Joy hadn't seen that coming. The defendant was entitled to a speedy trial, so his wishes might outweigh hers. She turned to Lance and said, "If the defendant is concerned about being able to post bond today, I am more than willing to work out bail with this judge."

Lance took her up on the offer. Bail was set for ten thousand and then Joy got back to her mission. "Now that we've handled that bit of business, I would like to reiterate the fact that I would like you to recuse yourself," she said to her father, the judge.

The defendant nudged Lance again. Lance spoke up again, "Your honor, if one of you has to go, my client would prefer that it be the prosecutor. He does not like the idea that his case would be delayed while he waits to be put on another judge's docket."

"What's his problem?" Joy asked indignantly. "If he makes bail, he'll be at home with his family and friends while he awaits a new trial date."

Lance turned back to Judge Marshall. "My client has a right to a speedy trial. His rights shouldn't be tossed aside at the whim of the prosecution."

Nelson turned to his daughter and said, "Well, Counselor?"

"Well what?" she snapped at her father, confused by the entire incident. Why on earth wouldn't a criminal be happy to have his court appearance moved back? He'd have more time to spend with his family and fellow criminal buddies before he is proven guilty and spends the next ten years behind bars.

"It looks like you're the one who needs to recuse," Nelson said to his daughter.

Joy threw up her hands, grabbed her briefcase and shouted, "Fine. You win. You always win!" She grabbed her purse and rushed out of the courtroom before she made a bigger spectacle of herself.

It just wasn't right. Her father was an awful human being, but things kept coming up roses for him. She wanted Nelson Marshall to pay for leaving her mother and ruining the family unit that she, her mother and brother had held dear. She had been a Daddy's girl, wanting to be just like Judge Nelson Marshall, for she had imagined that there was no greater human on earth than her dad. But that was before her father left her mother for Jasmine, her ex-friend, the skank. As a matter of fact, Jasmine had been Joy's roommate and her father had met Jasmine when Joy brought her over to the house for Sunday dinner.

As Joy reached the exit door, her head swiveled to the left as she spotted Jasmine seated in the last row of the courtroom. The woman had the audacity to roll her eyes at Joy as she looked her way. Joy wanted to reach across that aisle and go upside her head, the same way her mother had done to Jasmine years ago. But she reminded herself that she was in a courthouse and could get arrested for doing something like that.

Joy pushed open the door and walked out of the courtroom, and had almost made it out of the building when she heard Lance hollering behind her.

"Hey Joy, wait up."

She turned and waited for him to catch up. When he was standing in front of her she said, "Make it quick, Lance. I have a ton on my plate today."

"What happened in there? I've never seen you so frazzled."

Feeling foolish, she looked down at her feet and then glanced towards the wall behind Lance. She didn't owe him an explanation for her behavior. He wanted her to recuse herself and she did. That's it, end of story.

When Joy didn't respond he asked, "Is there anything I can do to help?"

"Yeah," she said, regaining her voice. "You can stay out of my business." With that she turned and left the building.

End of Excerpt...

About the Author

Vanessa Miller is a best-selling author, playwright, and motivational speaker. She started writing as a child, spending countless hours either reading or writing poetry, short stories, stage plays and novels. Vanessa's creative endeavors took on new meaning in1994 when she became a Christian. Since then, her writing has been centered on themes of redemption, often focusing on characters facing multi-dimensional struggles.

Vanessa's novels have received rave reviews, with several appearing on *Essence Magazine's* Bestseller's List. Miller's work has receiving numerous awards, including "Best Christian Fiction Mahogany Award" and the "Red Rose Award for Excellence in Christian Fiction." Miller graduated from Capital University with a degree in Organizational Communication. She is an ordained minister in her church, explaining, "God has called me to minister to readers and to help them rediscover their place with the Lord."

Vanessa has recently completed the For Your Love series for Kimani Romance and How Sweet the Sound for Abingdon Press, first book in a historical set in the Gospel era which releases March 2014. Vanessa is currently working on an ebook series of novellas in the Praise Him Anyhow series. She is also working on the My Soul to Keep series for Whitaker House.

Vanessa Miller's website address is:
www.vanessamiller.com But you can also stay in touch with Vanessa by joining her mailing list @ http://vanessamiller.com/events/join-mailing-list/ Vanessa can also be reached at these other sites as well:

Join me on Facebook: https://www.facebook.com/groups/77899021863/

Join me on Twitter: https://www.twitter.com/vanessamiller01

Vie my info on Amazon: https://www.amazon.com/author/vanessamiller

Made in the USA
Lexington, KY
20 July 2018